PEN~

## *In My Father's Den*

Maurice Gee is one of New Zealand's best-known writers, for both adults and children. He has won a number of literary awards, including the Wattie Award (twice), the Montana Award, and the New Zealand Fiction Award (four times). He has also won the New Zealand Children's Book of the Year Award. In 2003 he received an inaugural New Zealand Icon Award.

Maurice Gee's novels include the three books in the *Plumb* trilogy, *Going West* (winner of the Wattie award), *Prowlers*, *Live Bodies* (winner of the Montana Award) and *The Scornful Moon*. He has also written a number of children's novels, the most recent being *The Fat Man*, *Orchard Street* and *Hostel Girl*.

Maurice lives in Wellington with his wife Margareta and has two daughters and a son.

Also by Maurice Gee

**NOVELS**
The Big Season
A Special Flower
Games of Choice
Plumb
Meg
Sole Survivor
Prowlers
The Burning Boy
Going West
Crime Story
Loving Ways
Live Bodies
Ellie and the Shadow Man
The Scornful Moon

**STORIES**
A Glorious Morning, Comrade
Collected Stories

**FOR CHILDREN**
Under the Mountain
The World Around the Corner
The Halfmen of O
The Priests of Ferris
Motherstone
The Fireraiser
The Champion
Orchard Street
The Fat Man
Hostel Girl

# IN MY FATHER'S DEN

*Maurice Gee*

PENGUIN BOOKS

PENGUIN BOOKS

Published by the Penguin Group

Penguin Group (NZ), cnr Airborne and Rosedale Roads, Albany,
Auckland 1310, New Zealand

Penguin Books Ltd, 80 Strand, London, WC2R 0RL, England

Penguin Group (USA) Inc., 375 Hudson Street, New York, NY 10014, United States

Penguin Group (Australia), 250 Camberwell Road, Camberwell,
Victoria 3124, Australia

Penguin Books Canada Ltd, 10 Alcorn Avenue, Toronto,
Ontario, Canada M4V 3B2

Penguin Books (South Africa) (Pty) Ltd, 24 Sturdee Avenue, Rosebank,
Johannesburg 2196, South Africa

Penguin Books India (P) Ltd, 11, Community Centre, Panchsheel Park,
New Delhi 110 017, India

Penguin Ireland Ltd, 25 St Stephen's Green, Dublin 2, Ireland

Penguin Books Ltd, Registered Offices: 80 Strand, London, WC2R 0RL, England

First published by Faber and Faber, 1972
This edition first published by Penguin Group (NZ), 2004
7 9 10 8 6

Copyright © Maurice Gee, 1972

The right of Maurice Gee to be identified as the author of this work in terms of
section 96 of the Copyright Act 1994 is hereby asserted.

Printed in Australia by McPherson's Printing Group

ISBN 0 14 301941 4

A catalogue record for this book is available
from the National Library of New Zealand.

www.penguin.co.nz

*For Margaretha*

# Contents

Prologue 9

1928–1937 13

May 12, 1969 26

1938–1945 43

May 13–16, 1969 61

1945–1949 83

1949–1967 101

1968–1969 127

May 16, 1969 144

May 17, 1969 159

Epilogue 175

# Prologue

*Auckland Express,* May 13, 1969

## WADESVILLE GIRL STRANGLED

### Children's Grim Discovery

The strangled body of a seventeen-year-old schoolgirl was found hidden in a patch of scrub at Wadesville's Cascade Park late yesterday afternoon. The discovery was made by three young boys who were returning home from a Boys Brigade meeting. Police investigations began immediately.

The girl was identified as Celia Joan Inverarity, a pupil of Wadesville College. Her parents, Mr. and Mrs. C. B. Inverarity, live at 24 White Horse Road, Wadesville. They are well known in local business circles.

In charge of inquiries is Detective Inspector P. G. Farnon of Auckland C.I.B. Late last night he told our reporter that no clue to the identity of the murderer had been discovered. Police and dogs have been called in from Auckland and Hamilton and this morning a massive search will be conducted in the Cascade Park area. During the night inquiries were made among the residents of houses overlooking the park. Inspector Farnon is seeking information about the dead girl's movements in the period before 5 p.m. yesterday afternoon. He is also anxious to interview the driver of a blue or green Morris or Austin Mini seen in the vicinity of Cascade Park during the afternoon.

Celia was last seen alive by Mr. P. E. Prior, a master at Wadesville College. According to Mr. Prior she called on him at 3 p.m. at his home in Farm Road about a mile and a half from Cascade Park in order to return some books he had lent her. She left Mr. Prior's home at 4.15 p.m. and was not seen again until 5.15 when three nine-year-old boys discovered her body pushed into scrub at the edge of a clearing about fifty yards from the main track to the tidal pool at Cascade Park.

Inspector Farnon believes that Celia was probably knocked unconscious before she was strangled. Her face and body were heavily bruised. No further information about the nature of the attack is likely until a pathologist's report has been made. However, it appears that the murderer made a hasty attempt to hide the body. It was lying face up with its limbs neatly arranged. Several small trees had been bent forward to conceal it. But for the chance of the boys using the path it might have remained undiscovered for days or even weeks.

## STRANGLED GIRL WAS BRILLIANT SCHOLAR

Teachers at Wadesville College where murder victim Celia Inverarity was a pupil agree that the dead girl was the most promising scholar to attend the school in its seventeen year history. In 1967 Celia gained her School Certificate with the third highest marks of any pupil in the Auckland area. Last year she was accredited with her University Entrance examination and this year would have been a candidate for a University Scholarship.

Interviewed last night the headmaster of the college, Mr. E. Price, said Celia was a quiet unassuming girl with a ready sense of humour. Although she took little part in sport she belonged to several clubs in the school and had a lively interest in botany and music. There could be no doubt she had had a brilliant scholastic future.

Mr. Paul Prior, the dead girl's English teacher, said he had been asked by the police not to discuss his interview with Celia yesterday afternoon. She had called on him to return books he had lent her. He expressed shock and horror at the manner of Celia's death and agreed that she had been a brilliant scholar. Asked to name the books the girl had returned to him Mr. Prior declined to name the titles. They were connected with her English course, he said.

Neighbours of the Inverarity family were last night stunned and horrified at the news of Celia's murder. "She was a lovely girl, a lady," said one.

Another neighbour, who asked that his name be withheld, expressed anger that the Wadesville Borough Council had not cleared the area of scrub where Celia's body was found. "It's a menace to the community," he said, "and something should be done about it." In 1962 a young woman was criminally assaulted there by an attacker who was never identified. In 1966 it was the scene of a gang rape that resulted in five young men being sent to prison. And as recently as Christmas 1968 the clearing where Celia was apparently murdered became the headquarters of an Auckland motor-cycle gang that terrorized Wadesville for three days. "Now perhaps something will be done," said the neighbour, "but a girl's life is a high price to pay."

Last night as news of the crime became known a mood of grief and anger spread through the normally quiet little suburb of Wadesville. Groups of residents met in streets and in private homes. There was talk of forming a vigilante committee. Celia was one of their own. Her death is mourned, and if the people of Wadesville have any say in the matter it will not go unavenged.

## 1928–1937

I was born at the end of a gay decade in a small town called Wadesville, later to be a "quiet" suburb of Auckland. My father was fifty-three when I was born. He worked the apple and pear orchard he had planted after the First War. Father was a failed lawyer, a Presbyterian for the sake of household peace, a leaner towards free thought. (At his funeral a Unitarian friend of his described him to me as a Rationalist *manqué* and, less accurately, a scholar-hermit.) His years of manhood were a struggle for privacy—no less desperate for being secret—first from his housekeeper sister Jane, then from my mother. Mother was a plain, prim, thoughtful woman whose Sunday acquaintance with Jane had ripened, on her part at least, into friendship. She grieved for sour Jane when she died ("a wasting disease") and imagined Father helpless and lonely. They were married in 1927. In the wedding photograph my father looks sheepish and my mother determined. I was born in 1928, when she was nearly forty.

I was christened Paul Emerson Prior. Emerson was mother's maiden name, which Father was pleased to have me bear for a reason he thought it wise not to mention to her. It gave me the initials P.E.P. and doomed me as a teacher to the nickname Pepsi.

Mother I have said was plain. This is hindsight. I found her beautiful. She had a broad face that seemed to owe little to her Scottish ancestry. The bone structure has been made familiar by the Dalmatians who brought vineyards to the Wadesville valley early in the century. One of my brother Andrew's jokes, a fond joke, was to call her Mrs. Priorich. Her hair was brown and wavy and no amount of tying could make it severe. Half a dozen times a day she would pull it back from her face and ears in a way that to me seemed cruel, murmuring angrily all the time, and knot it tightly on her neck, but somehow it always escaped again. I believe she was secretly proud of it. It was only after John's birth that she cut it short.

My mother's vice was spirituality. Father used to say to us boys that she had a great soul. (His was the last generation that could make statements of that sort without irony.) My mother did not agree with his estimate. She knew her soul was of the common grey. Her life was a struggle to scrub it clean. One of the dim understandings of my childhood was that mother was less kind than good. It seems to me now that her struggle to improve her soul spoiled her kindness.

Her Presbyterianism was grim and fundamental. My religious education caused me little but confusion. I did not have Andrew's literal mind. Our moral training though had something of the quality of poetry. Mother put everything to use: insects, birds, plants, people, weather. At three or four, in neat grey home-sewn trousers, I knelt on a wet lawn after a thunderstorm watching a thin pink worm brought up by the rain, wondering whether he was Right or Wrong. And was the fly in the web being punished? What had the spider done to deserve him? What was the busy ant's reward? And the tree's on the bank for hanging on so tightly? If I owe my figurative habit of mind to this training I also owe a kind of moral hesitation—compounded now in my middle age by simple laziness. I yawn and turn away. If I am moved to seek an excuse for myself

14

I find it easily enough (lazily) in Mother's none too gentle bullying. "There is only one right way. One way. Paul," she would say to Andrew, "has a lazy soul. We must help him make it work. God only loves souls that work."

One day I found threepence and brought it home to show my parents. After asking me where I had found it my father told me I could put it in my money-box. But Mother had already slipped into what I later came to call High Gear. Her shoulder blades were sharpened as she stood at the stove, her neck was stiff, and her ears had turned a girlish pink. She faced me, without movement of her feet it seemed, as though a disk had rotated in the floor, and my hand with the threepence on it was drawn by a force like magnetism up to the level of her eyes.

"Did you try to find the owner, Paul?" she asked.

"No."

"Then it could belong to anyone in the street?"

"Yes."

"What do you think you should do?"

She often questioned us like this—a kind of testing of the moral circuits. Her disappointment when we were grossly wrong threw a greyness over the house that lasted till bed-time prayers, when all would be explained.

I thought desperately. "Put it in the plate next Sunday?" This was surely right, but I spoke with bitterness. I had never had threepence before.

"No," she said gently.

"Take it round the houses," my brother Andrew said. Although he was only five he had a skill in understanding her that seemed to me the result of cheating—I could not see how he did it.

"That's right Andrew," my mother said. "Paul must take it round the houses until he finds the owner."

I went out. I took the threepence round the houses. But I knocked on only one door. The man said, "Threepence?

Put it in your money-box, Paul." I looked at several other doors and could not make myself knock on them. My six-year-old mind had grasped that the business was ridiculous. So I dropped the threepence in a gutter and ran home fast to tell my mother I had dropped it in a gutter. She was angry but not suspicious. I bent my mind so strenuously to belief in that partial truth that I uttered it as a whole truth. Later I suffered from guilt. Every day I looked at the three-pence lying in the gutter. Beside it was an empty cigarette packet with a cloaked top-hatted man on it whom I took for a wicked angel sent to gloat over me. The coin stared up like an eye that never blinked—a magic eye, invisible to everyone but me. I suffered dreadfully and I prayed to God to make it go away. It stayed in the gutter until Sunday. Then a shower of rain washed it away. God had taken pity on me. I was delighted with Him and in a matter of seconds forgave my mother.

After this I began to enjoy guilt the way one can enjoy a toothache. I began to steal; then added cruelty to my sins. The orgy of pleasure and remorse I enjoyed one afternoon after school remains unequalled in my life for depth of emo-tion. I had stolen a packet of five dozen pink and blue cake papers from the grocery store. (I had taken them for Mother of course, but would never give them to her. It was a kind of spiritual gift.) I carried them in my shirt to the first of the three small waterfalls from which Cascade Park takes its name. There I launched them one by one and sailed them over the fall. A sort of continuous creation took place —I began to think of doomed sailors. So through the after-noon I launched them: pink and blue ships manned by spiders, caterpillars, beetles and small ti-tree jacks. All bound for a watery grave. My pleasure was intense. I imagined insect shrieks, families bereaved; I held down punishing monsters, black and toothed, that tried to crawl from the water. That night I confessed—I had not doubted

I would confess. Mother, stern and loving, wiped the tears from my face with her handkerchief and spoke of the smudge that must be washed from my soul. "Smudge" seemed inadequate to my sin. I continued to weep and concealed my disappointment. It was the only time her teaching failed through gentleness.

At other times she bore down so heavily upon me that I hated her. Once I transferred my love to my teacher. Miss Weaver had blonde fluffy hair and a face that hid all its bones. The older pupils said she looked like Claudette Colbert. Miss Weaver played favourites. She was, I realize now, a very bad teacher. Her favourites queued up at the end of each day to kiss her plump powdered cheek. My mother had burned my comic books. To underline my hatred of her I joined Miss Weaver's queue. Mother smelled of carbolic soap. Miss Weaver smelled of a perfume that made me think of angels. I licked my lips, tasted her powder, and fell in love with her.

The next morning before school someone sneaked into the classroom and bit Miss Weaver's shiny red apple. Was it me? To this day I don't know. It might have been. Perhaps I meant to express my love in this way. She took it as a kind of rape. The bite was crooked. Miss Weaver inspected teeth. My teeth were crooked. In tears I swore that I had not bitten her apple. I had hundreds at home, I said, thousands. I had my own apple in my bag. But Miss Weaver needed revenge. She held my mouth open for the class to see. See? Crooked teeth. Who else in the class had crooked teeth? Paul Prior must be taught not to tell lies. He must be taught not to bite other people's property. Miss Weaver strapped me. Then she took from her purse a tiny pearl-handled knife and publicly cut the crooked bite off the apple. She dropped it in the rubbish tin. The class hissed softly with pleasure. My tears stopped and my love was replaced by a deep implacable hatred. That night I could not eat my tea. Mother thought I was sick. She was kind to me but I was in an unforgiving mood. It was Father I told the story to, leaving out only the love bits.

The next day Mother came to the school. I saw her walk across the playground—Sunday hat, gloves, shiny purse—and I became an ostrich. I buried my head in my exercise book and tried to blot out the world. Darkness. The sound of Mother's knuckles rapping the door fell like the strokes of a cane. Miss Weaver strode across the room with her blackboard pointer couched on her arm like a lance. If she had run Mother through I would not have minded.

"I don't think you understand our problems, Mrs. Prior."

Mother replied, "I think I do, Miss Weaver. I taught at this school for sixteen years."

I had heard about angry fathers punching teachers on the jaw. It came to me suddenly that Mother was punching Miss Weaver on the jaw—in a kindly way, a Christian way. "I wonder if you've forgotten that in British countries a person is innocent until he's proven guilty."

Miss Weaver who had been so pretty became fat and ugly. "But the teeth marks were crooked," she managed to say.

"Surely that's circumstantial. There must be other children in the school with crooked teeth."

My mother did not ask Miss Weaver to say she was sorry. But Miss Weaver said it, facing me, reciting the words like a lesson. "I'm sorry Paul Prior. Perhaps I was a little bit hasty." Mother said, "Thank you," and went away. She had not looked at me once.

"That was my Mum," I said to the boy behind me.

Miss Weaver trembled for the rest of the lesson. I felt sorry for her but did not rejoin the kissing queue. I loved my mother again.

Father was of a coarser grain. He was more intelligent than Mother. The rules of conduct that governed her life were moral though she believed them religious. My father's conduct was tried less against a puritan conscience, though he too suffered from this, than a heretical belief, kept secret from his wife, that man is perfectable. He was unlucky to be born a Presbyterian. His mind was eclectic by nature and was crippled by a closed system. When he broke free late in his life he was able to travel no further than across town to the Unitarians. Nevertheless, for a man with his beginnings it was a brave journey.

It was not my father's spiritual backslidings that upset Mother. She did not learn how serious they were until her last years. His physical grossness was her greatest trial. She did not wish to know about ugly things and had developed turning away to a mode of conduct. But she could not turn away from my father. There was dirt ingrained in his hands. His shirts stank from sweaty days in the orchard. Hair sprouted from his nose and ears. While he sat in his chair waiting for dinner his stomach rumbled like a railway bridge. And his bathroom hawking and spitting—Mother had a way of turning the radio up to full volume even when all she could get was jazz. There was a kind of desperation in the way she would say to Andrew and me, "Your father is a good man." It was not enough. When she caught me hiding in the hedge by the dunny where he was trumpeting away like a Salvation Army band she slapped my face. She pressed her hands over my ears and rushed me down the path to the safety of her kitchen. I was crying in a corner when my father came in a few minutes later.

"Hallo Paul, have you been in the wars?" He came to stroke my hair.

"Henry, wash your hands," my mother said.

He patted me and went to the bathroom, and the top of my head where his hand had touched began to itch like a boil. My mother said, "Remember Paul, your father is a good man."

19

They were united in public; an ideal if old-fashioned couple. At home they were friendly. My father loved my mother though he seemed to have few ways of showing it. But the demon of godliness would not let her rest. She tried to keep her torment from us but always it broke out, destroying Father's peace and my enjoyments. "Edith," he would say, "your God has become a consuming fire." She moved towards stricter observances as he moved away. The prayers and kitchen parables and readings from the Bible that had always been a part of our lives became more and more of a trial to him. His mind was ranging widely, in a cautious way. Several times he tried to draw Mother with him but she withdrew from the edge of his discovered countries as though from a red light district. Once he came to her in the kitchen and said, "Have you seen my book, Edith?" Without a word she pointed to the stove. My father's face went lumpy. He fought with himself for a moment while Mother watched, righteous and cold. Then he smiled and said, "A consuming fire," and left the room. He told me years later it was Walt Whitman's *Leaves of Grass* she had burned.

I remember a happy afternoon. Our parents had taken us to play on the swings at Cascade Park. We ate sandwiches off a red-and-white cloth and drank orangeade. Father swung Andrew and me until our bodies lay flat on the air but Mother did no more than call to him to be careful. Danger to our limbs worried her less than danger to our souls. We ran into the bush and crept back like Indians. "Walla, walla, walla. Heap white squaw."

"Go away boys. You're tangling my hair."

We ran off towards the other end of the park. And this was the freedom I had been working towards. Buses had drawn up there, an organized picnic was under way. It was a tricky business not to alert Mother but my cunning held and from less than fifty yards away we watched the tug-of-war and the nail-driving competition. A man (was he fat and jolly?) called out to us, "Come on you two. You can join in." He threw great handfuls of lollies into the air, where they hung for a moment like stars.

Andrew said, "We'd better not." A lolly fell at his feet.

"That one's yours," I said.

We scrambled politely, with success. I had won four lollies, Andrew two, before we heard our mother calling us. Sucking hard, we went back to the red-and-white cloth.

"What are you eating?" she said.

"Lollies."

"We won them in the lolly scramble."

"They said we could."

"Just this once, Edith," my father smiled.

"I'm not sure. It doesn't seem right. . . ."

"We saw the tug-of-war," I cunningly said.

My father came to my help. "Whose picnic is it, Paul?"

I had read the name on a banner. Proud of the word, I said, "The Rationalists."

"Spit them out." Her hands were squeezing our cheeks. "Spit them out."

"Edith," my father said, "there can be no harm in the lollies."

"Spit them out."

We spat them out. She uncurled our fingers and marched the length of Cascade Park and flung our lollies into the pack of still-scrambling Rationalist children.

"Pack up, boys," my father said.

Crying, I asked, "What are Rationalists, Dad?"

"People who don't believe in God."

I was impressed. I stopped crying. "What do they believe in?"

"Lolly scrambles," he sighed.

"No really, Dad?"

He had a nervous eye on Mother, marching back towards

us. "Thinking about things. Making up their own minds. Some people call them free-thinkers."

"Do they think about God?"

"Yes. But they don't believe in Him. Help me with this table-cloth, Paul."

God must be biding His time, I thought. Or else it was all going on behind His back. But one day He'd turn round and see. Then they'd better look out. I was nervous until we were safely out of Cascade Park. But after that there was a little eddy of admiration in my mind when I thought of the Rationalists. The risk they were taking excited me.

It was in the next spring that my father came up from the orchard, smiling mysteriously, and said, "Come with me, boys." We followed him through the apple and pear trees to the fence that separated our property from the wild Catholic Flynns. There in a paddock the Flynns' cow Maggie was giving birth to a calf. (The Flynns were poor and dirty. During the depression Father had kept them supplied with bags of fruit. My mother approved but made sure our commerce with them went no further. Their dirt and "popery" were too much for her. The Flynn girls wore no shoes and, I think, no pants. Andrew and I believed they had fleas. Mr. Flynn drank. We had seen him fall off his bike. And in their house, or tumble-down shack, I had seen on my one apple-delivering visit a statue of Jesus with real thorns and drops of blood on His forehead. My mother went pale when I told her and said the Flynns were superstitious peasants.)

Now we stared at their cow giving birth. She was in a small hollow near the orchard fence. We stood on one side and three Flynn girls on the other. I remember being more interested in them at first than in the cow which was standing still doing nothing. It was a cold day and they stood in their washed-out dresses, without shoes or jerseys (or

22

pants), wiping their wet noses on their arms and staring impassively at Maggie. One of them had her feet in a cow pat.

"Look at her, Dad," I said.

He thought I meant the cow. "Watch. It's one of God's miracles."

I thought it was a long time coming. Maggie heaved but nothing happened. After a while she began to bellow. She went down on her knees and rolled on her side. Father saw something was wrong but he did not know what to do.

"It's one of God's miracles," he said again.

The cow's bellowing suddenly rose and quickened. It seemed like a sound that might come from a machine. The oldest Flynn girl started to run across the paddock. As she disappeared my mother arrived.

Her face was terrible. "Are you mad, Henry? Have you gone out of your mind?" she cried.

"It's the miracle of birth," he said. There was a lameness in his voice. He had not expected complications.

"Come with me Andrew. Paul," my mother said. She tried to pull us away from Father. We were only half aware of this. Maggie's tail was pointed towards us and something began to appear.

"Look," Andrew shrieked. He hid his face in my mother's dress. She pulled him towards the orchard. "Paul," she cried. Father had gripped my arm.

"I think he's old enough, Edith."

"Paul." My mother's voice seemed to call me from some terrible danger and I would have followed her, but Father's hand had gone right round my arm and he said, "I want him to see."

Mother took Andrew away. In a few minutes the Flynn girl and her mother ran out of their house and across the paddock. The girl fell behind—she was carrying a bucket and a bar of soap. Mrs. Flynn took one look at Maggie and

23

said to Father, "Are you useless, man?" She pushed up the sleeves of her jersey, ran to meet the girl, wet the bar of soap in the bucket and rubbed it on her arms. Then she came back to Maggie. She went down on her knees and pushed back into the cow whatever part of the calf it was that had been coming out. She wormed her arm deep into the cow's uterus. The calf's head came out then and the rest of it followed slowly. Mrs. Flynn pulled hideous faces. Once she made a cry of pain and changed her arm. The one she drew out was streaked with red. Then, as she kept on working, blood ran down her arm and dripped off her elbow. Suddenly it started to gush, as though from a tap. It splashed across the front of her dress and spread over the grass about her knees. "Lord save us," she cried.

Father told me Maggie had had a haemorrhage. There was nothing we could do—she would bleed to death. I watched her blood smoking lightly in the air, slipping like oil off the calf and seeping into the ground.

"Will the calf live, Dad?"

"It looks a bit crushed to me."

Mrs. Flynn picked it up and walked across the paddock to her house. One of her daughters started to cry. A moment later the mother came back, her wet dress clinging to her knees. She emptied the bucket of water and knelt by Maggie to see if she could get some milk for the calf. "What are we going to do now?" she said to my father.

We went up slowly through the orchard. The apple and pear blossoms were out and the air was heavy with the sound of bees.

"Did God make a mistake?" I asked.

"He doesn't make mistakes."

"But you said it was one of His miracles. And the cow died."

"I don't know, Paul. I think He only looks after the big things and the little things look after themselves."

"But what about the sparrows, and the hairs of our head?"

He changed the subject. He told me the Flynn girl had put her feet in the cow pat to keep them warm. This was interesting enough to take my mind off theology. I agreed that we should be kind to the Flynns. Every night after that my father or I met the oldest girl at the back fence and gave her a billy of milk from our own cow. The calf had died, Mary Flynn said. Her mother was making a mat from its skin. They had eaten the meat because it was "extra tender".

Very quickly it seems I became my father's child. Andrew remained my mother's. When I was nine years old my brother John was born. He was a mongoloid idiot. Mother brought him home from the hospital and put him down to sleep in the bassinet that had been first mine, then Andrew's. While my father watched she cut off her hair.

## May 12, 1969

I watched Celia walk away down Farm Road. Her sandals made a clacking sound on the tar-seal. To please her parents she had worn a dress suitable for Sunday walking—a grey Quakerish thing with long sleeves and a buttoned collar. Her hair fell down her back to the level of her shoulder-blades. It was brown and straight and newly washed. There had been a faint piney smell about her that was neither perfume nor soap. I thought of the struggles she had had with poor Miss Selwyn. Unbecoming: Silly's favourite word. She was always at Celia to cut her hair, tie it, torture it somehow. Becoming was the word I thought of as I watched her walk down the road. Sunlight slanted across the valley and shone on the calves of her legs. Her gleaming hair was like a Crusader's hauberk of chain mail.

At the corner she turned and waved. She went into the scurfy patch of ti-tree and stunted pine the road winds through before it climbs the hill towards the Great North Road.

She had kissed me lightly on the cheek. I thought with a grave fondness that the danger she was so careless of was mine rather than hers; reminding myself that she was a child, not a woman. I went inside. In my den the shivery grass she had brought me stood in a vase on one of the bookshelves. She was not a flowery girl and liked to pick things at the roadside or in the bush. She had also brought a handful of prickly dull-green leaves—a herb, she thought. We had spent part of her visit trying to identify them in a botanical encyclopaedia. I sat down and picked up my book. I was reading *The First Circle* and as I read of the sufferings of Nerzhin and Rubin I nibbled the leaves. They had a faintly eucalyptic taste. I could not believe they were poisonous: about plants I had never known Celia wrong.

I was still reading at half-past six when Jim Beavis telephoned me. "Paul? Have you heard the news about Celia Inverarity?" Jim Beavis teaches science at Wadesville College. I thought at once of triumphs for Celia: scholarships, prizes—at least some brilliant paper she had turned in.

"She's been murdered. Strangled. They found her body at Cascade Park. It's a madhouse down there, boy. The place is swarming with police."

I don't remember what I did. There was a moment of primitive consciousness: I floated in my murky room like some creature in the sea, aware only of a chair and a book in a globe of light from the reading lamp.

I said, "Who did it?"

"They don't know. They haven't caught anyone yet. Some kids saw a car by the scrub. That's where they found her, in the scrub that motor-bike gang used at Christmas."

"Whose car?"

"Whoever strangled her, I suppose. The police will find out, no doubt about that. You should see the organization they've got down there. Fantastic."

"She was strangled?"

"That's what they think. Knocked around pretty badly too. You know, punched and kicked. He must have been a maniac, eh? A real bloody monster—pervert."

"Was she raped?"

"Don't know. It's my guess she was. What else would anyone do it for?" He laughed; a high squeaking sound. I saw how excited he was and I put down the phone. But at once I grabbed it again. "Jim, Jim." I wanted to ask were they sure, were they absolutely sure it was her. The connection had been broken. I put the phone back again and went to my chair.

I was still holding some leaves of the herb Celia had brought me. I emptied them on my open book. Two or three had stuck to my palm and I brushed them off with the tips of my fingers. I put the book on the coffee table and sat in my chair. These were deliberate acts. Then there was nothing left to do. My mind went wild with fictions: it was not Celia, some other girl; she fought her attacker off, ran through the scrub. . . . But my body knew the truth. I sweated. The sweat had a goatish smell it had never had before.

When I heard a car draw up outside the house I ran to the lavatory. In the tiny room, with the white pan and black seat, I managed to exclude the world. I crouched down and pressed the palms of my hands on the ice-cold porcelain. I tried to take the coldness into my mind as the fact of Celia's death. Isolation was a state I had made natural to myself, and the private shaping of emotions was, I had believed, my special skill; but now, like Volodin in his cell, I found an official eye looking in: my own. I saw myself posturing, and I stood up, making an exclamation of anger. Self-disgust I had long since given up, but I felt a kind of rage at my trickiness. Celia was dead!

Footsteps sounded on the veranda and a thick unhurried knocking on the door.

"Hang on," I called.

I washed my hands in the bathroom and found myself wondering at the act. It seemed impossible that everything was not now standing still. How could we go on? I go on? I wanted to shout these questions down the hall to whoever it was standing on the porch.

The knocking came a second time. I called that I was

coming. My voice had a shrill tone of complaint. I went down the hall and opened the door.

"Mr. Prior?" said the man on the veranda.

"Yes." He was tall, narrow-faced, with a nose like a parrot's beak and a mouth childishly pursed. His eyes were sharp and watery, like those of an old lady peering at fancy work.

"I'm Farnon. Detective-Inspector." He inclined his head at the man standing beside him. "This is Detective-Constable Glover."

"Yes?"

"We're inquiring into the death of one of the pupils at your school."

"Celia Inverarity," I said.

"Ah, you know."

"I had a telephone call."

I showed them into the den and told them to sit down. Farnon's body behaves like Jacques Tati's, but there was something frightening in clumsiness at this moment, something too human. He made no move towards a chair. Glover stood in a head-boy way at his side.

"Do you usually have it this dark?"

I turned on the light and turned off the reading lamp. They watched me closely. "You don't think I did it?" I said.

"We have to make inquiries, Mr. Prior. I'm sure you understand."

"Of course."

"Would you tell me who rang you?"

"Jim Beavis. He teaches at the school."

Glover had a flip-pad out. He started to write and at this I thought wildly, Christ, Jim Beavis did it. I was overcome by a hatred that must have shown on my face. Farnon said, "What is it?"

"I was wondering how he knew. But of course, he lives by

29

Cascade Park." The name was a trigger (it still is). "How did it happen? How did she get there?"

"That's what we're trying to find out, Mr. Prior."

"Is it true whoever did it kicked her?" I was thinking of pointed shoes but found them replaced as I spoke by the heavy round-toed ones of a middle-aged man—like the pair Farnon was wearing. I saw him glance at my feet as I looked at his and he gave a dry smile. I was wearing slippers.

"We have to wait for a report."

"From the pathologist?"

"That's right. Now, about this fellow Beavis?"

I told him what Jim had said. "Rape?" said Farnon, sliding his eyebrows back into the hollow of his forehead.

"He said he couldn't imagine any other reason."

Glover wrote.

"Was she raped?"

"We don't know. What would you guess?"

"Robbery? But she had nothing."

"No purse? No bracelets or rings?"

"Nothing. Her parents must have told you." I thought about Charlie and Joyce then. And I looked at Farnon with awe. He must have come from talking with them. "How are they taking it?"

"About how you'd expect."

"I know the Inveraritys."

"She's hysterical. He's in a state of shock." There seemed to be something flippant in the remark. I looked at him sharply, but the lightness in his voice was his first sign of anger. He was watching me with an interest more than clinical. "They told me she came to see you."

"She brought back some books. I'm a suspect, aren't I?"

"Was it normal for you to have pupils here?"

"No."

"Just Celia?"

"I gave her special coaching. Not book-work. I just

talked to her. She's the best English pupil I've ever had."

"Was, Mr. Prior."

"Yes, was." He waited. "Price said to get the parents' permission. He said to be careful."

"The headmaster?"

"Yes."

"Why would you need to be careful?"

"Celia was seventeen. She was an attractive girl."

"And you're not married?"

"No."

"Any reason?"

"I've never wanted to be."

Farnon nodded. "Got that, Bob?" I took out my handkerchief and wiped my hands and face. Again I caught the smell of my sweat and I wondered if it was reaching Farnon. He was looking at my handkerchief. I knew at once he wanted to see bloodstains. I held the handkerchief out to him, and saw that this was a wrong move—what need should I have to think as fast as they? He held it up by the corners. Except for the marks of my sweat it was clean.

"What's the smell?"

"After-shave lotion. I always put a bit on the corner."

His mouth tightened. He handed the handkerchief back. "What time did she get here this afternoon?"

"A bit before three. About ten-to."

"Did she have anything except the books?"

"Some shivery grass. And some wild herbs." I pointed to the leaves lying on my book. Farnon had already seen them. He looked instead at the grass in the vase. "Where does that grow?"

"All along the road. She could have got it anywhere."

He nodded at the leaves. "What about these?"

"There's an old shack down in the hollow. Derelict. The kids call it the haunted house. These were growing in the garden."

Farnon nodded. "What I'm trying to get at is whether she met anyone on the way, or arranged to meet him afterwards." He had taken me on to his side. I watched him suspiciously. "Was she a good girl?"

"Yes."

"Moral?"

"Yes. I'm sure of it."

Glover made a note of my certainty.

"Did she go with boys?"

"That's ambiguous." I was angry, but he gave a faint smile and said, "Did she have a boy-friend?"

"Not that I know of."

"Was she a virgin?"

"How would I know? Why don't you wait for your pathologist's report?"

"It wasn't the sort of thing you talked about?"

"No. It wasn't."

"You talked about books?"

"Yes."

"Schoolwork?"

"Yes."

"Her personal life?"

"A bit."

"Would you say you were more than a teacher to her?"

"I was a friend."

"How much of a friend?"

"A good friend. A close friend. She was fond of me."

"And sometimes you talked about her personal life. Was there anyone who hated her? Or for that matter liked her especially?"

"I liked her." A simple statement and it made me cry. I held my handkerchief to my mouth and sobbed, while Farnon watched with curiosity and, I think, a small amount of pleasure.

I asked if I could go to the bathroom. I splashed cold

water on my face and then stripped off my shirt and singlet and washed the top half of my body. I had not cried since my father's death. The white face and red eyes looking at me from the mirror were shrunken and old but somehow like a very young man's. I told myself I should be past grief and past self-pity. My pose was detachment, which long practice had made the real thing. Until Celia. My eyes filled with tears again. Angrily I splashed more water on my face. As I reached for the towel I saw Farnon standing at the door watching me.

"I wasn't going to run away."

He was looking at my chest and arms—looking for scratches. I turned round so he could see my back. Slowly I dried myself and hung up the towel. There were noises in my bedroom and I guessed Glover was there. Farnon heard them too. "I thought you wouldn't mind if we had a look round. It's routine."

I put on my singlet and shirt and went back to the den. He followed me. "Could we go on, Mr. Prior?"

I sat down. "There wasn't anyone who hated her. And apart from me I don't know anyone who liked her especially. She wasn't a mixer."

"What about friends? At school?"

"She wasn't in any clubs. She didn't play sports. She liked reading and walking and listening to music. She liked weeds." I motioned at the shivery grass. "And spiders. And things you find under rocks. She liked flute music, and Breughel, and Chinese poetry."

"This is interesting——"

"She was collecting. She was busy becoming someone. Words. She loved words. Her latest one was 'prodigious'. She used it every chance she got."

"All right. Now about school——"

"Price didn't like her. She refused to be a prefect."

"Any reason for that?"

"She said she had no intention of being a policeman."

Farnon sighed. "How did you feel about it?"

"I supported her. Price doesn't like me either."

"Are there many people who don't like you?"

"I've never bothered to find out."

Glover was in the kitchen. I heard him open the back door and go outside.

"What's he trying to find?"

"We'll come to that, Mr. Prior. This personal life you talked about with Celia—what was it?"

"Her parents. Her father. He wanted her to leave school and get a job. A good old-fashioned type, Charlie. He doesn't believe in education for girls."

"How did she feel about that?" He was simply keeping me talking, giving Glover time.

"Nothing was going to stop her. She was going to university. The crazy degree she wanted to do. Music, botany, Chinese. . . . She was sorry for Charlie."

"Why sorry?"

"The marriage wasn't working. They slept in separate rooms."

Farnon widened his eyes. I saw that I had shocked him. "She told you that?"

"Why not?"

He went to the window and looked outside. Glover was busy at the garage. I heard the door scrape on the gravel drive. Farnon turned suddenly. "So there were no boys?"

"Not really. Just casual things."

"Or men?"

"No."

"Except you." His shock had given way to angry distaste. "What did you talk about this afternoon?"

"Books. These." I pushed the herbs with my finger. "We tried to find out what they were in an encyclopaedia." I remembered her saying that her father had bought a set of encyclopaedias at the door—they were the only books he owned and although he never opened them he sometimes tapped their spines possessively. Typical of Charlie. As I thought this a suspicion went off in my mind like a flare, illuminating a picture I had treasured as comic: Charlie Inverarity, thirteen, spiky-haired, masturbating fiercely at a photograph of Betty Grable tacked to the trunk of a pine tree.

"He did it," I said. "Her father."

"What?"

"He wanted her. He wanted to go to bed with her."

Farnon came back from the window in a couple of strides. His head was lowered like a turkey's and his parrot nose stopped only inches from mine. I pushed myself into the back of the chair.

"You slimy little bastard," he said.

"She told me."

"Told you what?"

The image faded. I was lost. I managed a kind of Fagin shrug. "That he wanted her."

"Had he touched her? Had he made any move towards her?"

"She sensed it. It was a feeling."

"She sounds like a cheap little trollop to me."

I tried to push him away but he put his hand on my chest and held me in the chair. "Have you heard about corrupting a minor?"

I struggled to get up. He dug his thumb into my sternum. The pain made me cry out. Then, contemptuously, he took his hand away and stayed leaning close as though offering me a free chance to hit him. I saw Celia vanishing behind this badly-made face and I thought bitterly, it hasn't taken long, it's only taken an hour. Now she was just a name, a case—a memory anyone could cheapen. Someone I was in trouble over. Shakily I took out my handkerchief. I wiped

35

my face and hands. Trying to keep my voice steady I said, "I'm telling you this because it's what she said. It's something you've got to investigate."

Farnon straightened up and moved away from me.

"He could have done it," I said. "If you didn't have such a cut and dried mind you'd see that."

He sighed, putting on an air of weariness—calming himself. "We're not as stupid as you think."

"What do you mean?"

"Celia's father was playing golf all afternoon. He was still at the course when we called him." I heard the garage door scrape on the gravel again. "So we'll forget this little yarn of yours—and I mean *forget* it." He came forward and turned on the reading lamp. Glover came into the room. "Turn off the light, Bob." Glover turned it off. The reading lamp had a concentrated beam. I sat in this while Farnon and Glover moved dimly outside it.

They really think I killed her, I thought, and I said in a stupified way, "What's the matter?"

"I just thought you'd be more comfortable."

"You've got no right."

"If you've done nothing you're safe, Mr. Prior."

I began to babble. I tried to tell them nobody was safe, life was a trap, a torture machine, look what it had done to Celia, anything could happen, anything seem true.

Farnon ignored me. He lit a cigarette. "You talked about books," he said. "What then?"

"School."

"Anything else?"

"I read her a poem."

"What poem?"

"One of Garcia Lorca's."

"Who's he?"

I told them.

"Did you give her anything to drink?" Glover said.

My mind had a bruised feeling. I began to lie and could not stop even when I saw how they would trap me.

"No."

"Not even a cup of tea?"

"Yes, a cup of tea."

"Did you wash the cups?"

"Yes."

"Who was the visitor you had when she'd left?"

"I didn't have any visitor."

"You drank sherry with someone."

"I had a glass of sherry by myself."

"There are two glasses in the sink."

I sat in the puddle of light like a frog and stared out at these people who were poking me with sticks. I said nothing.

Farnon said, "How much sherry did you give her?"

"None," I said.

"We can finger-print the glasses."

"She asked for it. It wasn't my idea."

"How much?"

"One glass."

"Sure about that?"

"Yes. One glass. A small one."

"How much did you drink?"

"The same. A small glass." I was telling the truth now and was furious when I saw they didn't believe me. Farnon said, "We'll see, Mr. Prior. After you'd had this sherry what happened?"

"She went home."

"Why?"

"It was time. It was quarter-past four. Her mother wanted her home by half-past."

"It's two miles from here to her place."

"Yes."

"She wouldn't make it by half-past."

"No."

"Why didn't you offer to drive her?"

"I did. But she wanted to walk. She liked walking."

"What sort of car do you have, Mr. Prior?"

"A Morris Mini."

"What colour?"

"Green."

"Have you had it out today?"

"Yes. I went to the dairy this morning. For a *Sunday Times*."

"And what time this afternoon?"

"Not. Not at all. I haven't been out this afternoon."

"Beavis told you some boys saw a car at Cascade Park?"

I nodded, beginning to understand.

"Did he tell you what sort?"

"No."

"What would your guess be?"

I shook my head, but they waited. At last I said, "A Mini I suppose."

"That's right. A Mini. Can you guess the colour?"

"No." My voice was a whisper.

"What colour was it, Bob?" Glover leafed through his pad. He was a clumsier actor than Farnon. After a moment he said, "Ah, here it is. Two of them said it was green, and the other thought it might have been blue. I suppose it's the sort of colour people can't make up their minds about."

"I was home," I said. "I never left the house."

"Has Celia been in your car?"

"Not since last year. We went to Muriwai."

"What for?"

"Just for the trip. She hadn't been to a West Coast beach."

"And she hasn't been in the car since then?"

I shook my head. I couldn't remember, but made a kind of gambler's throw. If they found new finger-prints I knew they'd arrest me.

38

"Call Menzies," Farnon said, and Glover went out to the car. Farnon sat down on the sofa.

"Anything else you'd like to tell us?"

I shook my head.

"How long have you been at Wadesville College?"

"Six years." He wasn't really interested, he had put his mind in a kind of at-ease position.

"Where did you teach before that?"

I told him.

"Any family? Parents?"

"I've got a brother."

"Where's he?"

"On the North Shore. Takapuna."

Farnon almost yawned. But asking questions was a habit with him. "Celia's father told me you used to go to school with him."

"Yes."

"That makes you a local boy?"

"My father had an orchard here. Where the factories are now."

"What about Mrs. Inverarity?"

"She came after the war. I took her out a few times. Then she started going with Charlie and they stayed together until they got married."

He looked interested at this but did not ask the questions I expected. "What made you come back?"

"I was born here. It was time to stay in one place."

Glover came in. "He's on his way. There's a couple of reporters outside. The word seems to have got around that our friend was the last one to see her."

Farnon went out. In a few moments he beckoned me into the hall. "You say nothing. You tell them she was a nice girl and say how upset you are. Okay?"

I said yes and he let me go outside. The night and the air made me feel as if I was coming out of prison. The reporters were waiting half-way down the path. The one from the *Express* was a small middle-aged man with inquisitive eyes that seemed at the same time hurt and humble. He asked the questions while his companion from the *Telegraph* wrote and kept his eye on Farnon who was standing on the veranda. I told them I was shocked and horrified. I told them Celia had been a brilliant pupil. I could see they had guessed what was going on but were nervous of stepping off the line Farnon had drawn for them. He strolled down the path past us and watched the lights of a car coming down the hill towards the hollow.

"What's your opinion about how she was killed?"

"I don't have an opinion. Ask the Inspector."

"Where were you when it happened?"

"Here."

"How did you find out?"

I told them.

"What sort of girl was she? You know. Boy-friends. Things she did. Books she read."

"I don't know. I was only her teacher."

"You'd know about books. What about the ones she brought back today?"

Farnon was facing us and Glover was on the veranda. The car came up from the hollow and passed the place where Celia had waved to me.

"They were part of her English course."

"Did she read romances, that sort of thing?"

"No."

"Any little details, Mr. Prior. We're trying to get a picture of what the girl was like."

Farnon had a right to his questions. These men were taking Celia into a world where her death could be enjoyed. I told them I had nothing to say and I went inside. Glover followed me. As I went across the veranda the car stopped at the gate and Menzies the finger-print man got out. I sat down in my chair and Glover stood opposite, watching me.

"That was a good question," he said.

"What?"

"The books she brought back today."

I took them off the top of the low bookshelf by my chair and handed them to him. Breughel, Stanley Spencer, Hieronymus Bosch. I had let her explore without system. Glover leafed through the Breughel and Spencer. I could see he didn't like them. The cover of the Bosch was enough to make him look up sharply. He turned on the main light and sat down. When he came to *The Garden of Delights* I asked him if he would like a magnifying glass. He had very young blue eyes. "In your position I wouldn't joke." He stood up as Farnon came in. "These are the books he was lending her."

Farnon glanced at them. "Go and give Phil a hand." He looked through the books. "I thought you said they were part of her English course."

"It was none of their business."

"Doesn't pay to lie to journalists. Did she like them?"

"She liked Breughel and Spencer. She thought Bosch was a joke."

"Do you like him?"

"He's interesting."

"What do you feel about lending this sort of stuff to a seventeen-year-old?"

"It's in the school library. We've got a good art teacher."

"What else did she borrow?"

"Anything she liked. There were no restrictions."

He smiled at the tone of my voice. "Name something."

"Lawrence. She took a lot of Lawrence once."

"*Lady Chatterley's Lover ?*"

"Amongst others."

"You really are something, Mr. Prior."

"I'm good at my job, that's all."

41

We sparred for a while. I made myself ridiculous in a way I hadn't since student days. My talk of Philistines, "the precious life blood", book-burning and the jackboot, was a kind of defence against the trap that was closing. Noises came from the garage and later from the kitchen and bedroom. Menzies had a quiet voice that scared me.

At half-past ten Farnon and Glover had a talk in the hall. Farnon came back. "You can go to bed, Mr. Prior."

I had been so sure they'd arrest me that I sat and gaped at him.

"I'm going to leave a man here—just to keep a check on things. It's irregular but I don't think you'll mind."

"I thought you were going to arrest me."

Farnon gave his faint wise-child smile. "Get a good night's sleep."

"Can I have a bath?"

He shrugged. "You're a free man. Don't go anywhere though. We'll want to talk to you in the morning."

So Farnon and Glover left and a constable called Fernie sat in my den for the rest of the night. I boiled an egg and ran a bath. The soap more than anything made me think of Celia.

By midnight I was in bed. The day swelled like a bladder. It was stuffed with forms Bosch might have drawn. It pulsed at me like a jellyfish. I thought it was going to suck me in. Then I remembered that in the morning Farnon was coming back to arrest me. That gave me something to hold on to.

Shortly after lying down I went to sleep.

## 1938–1945

The business area of Wadesville lies between two bridges. The shopkeepers call it the "Golden Mile". Among the older ones conversation often turns to the fortunes that could have been made, and the few that were, in property deals. This talk takes place in an atmosphere almost religious—the familiar elements are there: virtue and vice (courage and timidity in this case), reward and punishment. But it seems to me that one would have had to be extremely clever or extremely stupid to want land in Wadesville in 1938. The town had hardly changed since the war. On the Great North Road between the bridges we had a butcher's shop, a baker's shop and bakehouse, a grocer's, a blacksmith's shed on its last legs, and a boarding-house that had been a pub before the area went dry. The main part of the town was on Railway Street opposite the station: a dozen shops and a concrete town hall that also served as a picture theatre.

My father's orchard lay between the town and one of the creeks. To reach school Andrew and I crossed a swing-bridge and went along a clay road at the side of a Dalmatian vineyard. The school was on a hillside sloping towards Wadesville. The Presbyterian Church stood across the valley on the road leading out.

Wadesville, my Wadesville of school, shopping centre, park, creek, came to know me well. I became a rough, tough character. I might have a loony brother but I showed my schoolmates there was nothing wrong with me. Charlie Inverarity was the other tough boy in my class. He was Earl McCready, I was Lofty Blomfield. We wrestled each other through a hot lunch-hour and lay at the end of it knotted so tightly together a teacher had to undo us. We circled each other warily after that and became friends because there was no other satisfactory ending. Charlie's idea was to run wild. He wanted to pillage, burn, and put to the sword. I held him back. Charlie had never been in a church in his life. My Presbyterian upbringing inclined me to tactics. I made sure we didn't hit the same orchard too often. I made sure that one of us kept watch while the other looked through the nail holes into the girls' changing shed at Cascade Park. I chose vineyards where the Dalmatians didn't use shotguns. We never got caught. I think this was a disappointment to Charlie.

One orchard we never raided was my father's. Charlie couldn't understand. Didn't he steal cigarettes from his old man? Didn't I help him smoke them? He salvaged something by helping me guard the orchard against other gangs. I was my father's now. My mother had folded herself in on John. There was a door to that world Andrew could open but I did not have the key. Nor did I often want to go in. My father was enough for me. He helped me build a hut in a tree, and later an underground one. He made me shanghais and bows and arrows. Mid-summer: I was in the creek or by it more often than at home. Father taught me how to make an eel trap. He gave Charlie and me sheets of corrugated iron and told us how to build canoes. We hammered out the corrugations, nailed in prow and stern posts, and sealed the cracks with boiling pitch. Early one Saturday we launched our canoes on the creek and set off on a voyage of discovery.

Today the creek is a sour ditch, scummy with factory waste. In those days it was green, mysterious, frightening, magic. I can travel down it in my mind, remembering each pool and mossy rock and fallen tree the way other people remember kind or cruel actions, women they have had or tries they have scored. Charlie and I struck out with our wooden paddles. We went under the swing-bridge and down a long stretch of Amazonian water. Once we saw a Dalmatian face grinning at us from the top of the bank, but we put down our heads, dug in our paddles, and wobbled on. We wanted to put faces behind us, we wanted crocodiles, boa constrictors. In the middle of the morning we found a drowned pig, with eels trailing from its underside like black streamers. We wondered what we would do if we found a body. We passed under the bridge that carried the Great North Road into Wadesville. It looked as if it had grown there. It had velvety red and green moss on its pillars and black fungus on its underside. We sat awed in our canoes and listened to cars rushing over it. We had cut ourselves off, there was no safety now, the world was in another place. We paddled on, quiet and hardy. When we had to speak we kept our voices low.

Near midday we sat on a mat of red willow-hair and ate our jam and Marmite sandwiches. The shouting of children came to us from Cascade Park. "Let's go fast," Charlie said. We paddled hard, made a portage round the waterfalls, and set off across the swimming pool, out of the reach of older boys who swam after us and threw stones. Now we were on the tidal part of the creek, on brown fish-smelling water. We paddled seawards through the afternoon, through farms and orchards, until the creek widened to an estuary and we had broad banks of mud and mangrove swamps on either side. Launches and yachts were moored in side-creeks, at wooden jetties at the foot of paddocks. Seagulls turned lazily overhead. At last we saw the sea. It was wide and silver, running into the mud. At the other side was the North Shore. On cliffs red with late afternoon sunlight stood pink and white houses whose windows burned like fires. We felt as if we had discovered a new civilization.

This was the happiest day of my life. I keep it safe by formalizing it: launching, fear, comradeship, discovery. Even the end was perfect. It was too late to go back. We tried to hide our canoes in the mangroves but could not pull them over the banks of mud. We sank in to our hips. So we left them there, side by side, half-way between the water and the land. The next tide must have floated them away. We ran home through the twilight like a pair of steeplechasers, wearing leggings of mud, and parted at the corner with cries of tomorrow's meeting and a shrill duet of whistles growing further apart.

My mother did not like Charlie Inverarity. I was careful not to bring him home too often. My father said, "Try not to bring your friends here, Paul. Your mother's not well and noise upsets her." He did not mention names. Charlie was tough, bony, cheeky. He had an ugly nasal voice that offended Mother's ear: her children had been taught to speak well. But worst of all he was the son of the local book-maker. Mr. Inverarity had a draper's shop by the station. Charlie explained to me one day as we sat on bolts of material reading comics that the people who came in and handed slips of paper across the counter were making bets. He said his mother took bets by telephone at home. I called on Charlie the next Saturday, hoping to see this perform-ance, and watched Mrs. Inverarity in dressing-gown and hair curlers write £1 win, 10/- pl. Red Monarch in an exercise book. She had a glass of beer on the edge of the book and a cigarette in her mouth. It wobbled up and down as she spoke. I thought of my own mother with her cropped hair, white face, far-away voice, moving about John's bassinet and my father escaping to the packing shed or orchard. The name Red Monarch floating up out of that time still brings me a thrill of freedom and—not danger, "peril".

One wet winter Saturday the police raided the Inverarity house. Mrs. Inverarity pushed Charlie out the back door with an armful of exercise books. "Run Charlie," she said. He went down the backyard and escaped through the hedge just as a constable ran round the corner of the house and started to hammer on the back door. He didn't know where to go from there so he ran down the hill towards school, down the clay road by the vineyard and over the swing-bridge. He arrived on our doorstep soaking wet with an armful of sodden exercise books just as we were finishing lunch. My father answered the door. "Paul," he called. I went to the door. "Take your friend down to the packing shed. I'll be down in a minute." I put on my oilskin and took Charlie down through the orchard. He was sniffing, gulping, shivering. Some of the water on his face was tears. We went into the packing shed. Charlie threw the books on to a pile of apple-boxes. "Bloody fucking things," he said. For the first time I saw that he had problems too. It made me like him less. The shed was like the inside of a refrigerator. The wind came up through the floor and ran up our legs like water. I offered Charlie my coat. "Keep it," he said, and he wrapped himself in a coal-sack he found in a corner.

A few minutes later my father arrived, wearing his oilskin and carrying a Gladstone bag. He handed me the bag, took a key from his pocket, and opened the door of the lean-to where he kept the insect and weed-killers. Andrew and I called it the poison-shed. We were not allowed inside. My father turned on a light. He stood in the doorway taking from the bag which I held open to him a towel, a pair of my trousers, a shirt and a jersey. "All right," he said, "come in."

Charlie and I went into the poison-shed. It was like a magic cave. Sure enough there were insecticides in a corner, neatly stacked. But there was a mat on the floor, a picture on the wall, a table, a cup, a packet of tea, a kettle with an electric plunger in it, an electric heater which my father turned on, a wooden carving of a wounded bear. Most amazing of all, there was a wall full of books. I had never seen so many books, not even in the Wadesville lending library.

Charlie stripped off and dried himself in front of the heater

47

while I looked around. My father seemed shy. "Do you like it, Paul?" he asked.

"Yes," I said, "it's—it's marvellous." My father went red with pleasure. He got very busy. "Right, my boy," he said to Charlie, "put these clothes on. I'll make you a cup of tea."

He closed the door and the poison-shed started to warm up. Charlie got into my clothes and drank a cup of tea with huge spoonfuls of sugar in it. My father sat in the chair watching us as we knelt in front of the heater. Charlie was interested in the bear and my father handed it down to him. It was rearing on its hind legs. The broken shaft of a spear was fixed in its chest. I see now why my father liked it but it puzzled me then. I knew he hated hurting things. So I handled the carving for a while, then gave it back to Charlie. I stared at the picture on the wall. A pre-dentist or pre-punishment feeling ran through me: the expectation of pain in which excitement plays a part. As I looked at the picture I felt that something more was on the point of being shown. I saw a woman in a white robe sitting on a globe meant to be the world. She was blind-folded and her hands were resting on an instrument, a harp I thought, with all the strings broken except one.

My father watched me.

"Is it supposed to be an angel?"

He shook his head. "*Hope*, Paul. It's a great work of art."

I didn't ask any more questions because even this explanation made the picture less mysterious. I looked at it from time to time as I went along the rows of books. The globe of the world was golden, with a misty sky behind it. The woman sat gracefully, with her head bent to listen. Her hand was poised to pluck the string. Would the last string break? All through the afternoon the question kept me tense. What would happen if it broke? My father read. Charlie played at spearing the bear. He brought in his mother's exercise books and tried to dry them in front of the heater. For a while he nosed about the poison but my father called him away. I read the titles of the books and was pleased they were too hard for me. In spite of Charlie and things like the tea and sugar the shed was still a magic cave. The titles added to the mystery. I spelled them out with care. *Man the Unknown. Cosmic Consciousness. Varieties of Religious Experience.* They were mostly old books. Some, when I took them down, had poetry in them. In the margins my father had written *Good! True! Rubbish!* Sometimes whole pages were underlined. I was proud of him. I kept smiling at his back. As if to reward me he underlined something in the book he was reading, and wrote in the margin. I sidled close. *But see p. 67.* The message haunts me still. For a long while I knew that p. 67 would tell me if the last string was going to break.

It stopped raining and Charlie went home. I asked my father if I could stay with him in the shed.

"I don't know if there's anything here you can read," he said. "Would you like to make me a cup of tea?"

I rinsed Charlie's cup and filled the kettle at the tap outside the shed. I made my father a cup of tea.

"Just a minute," he said. He went out to the packing shed and I saw him empty some rusty nails out of an old jam jar. He washed the jar and brought it back sparkling clean. "We'll give you one too."

So we drank tea, he from the cup, I from the jam jar, and later I ran up to the house to tell my mother we would be busy in the shed for the rest of the afternoon. As usual she was sitting in her chair watching John who was crawling about the floor. Andrew was busy with his Sunday School books. "I'm helping Dad in the shed," I sang out. I don't think she knew where the voice came from. "All right," she said, turning her head in a puzzled way. I ran back through the wet grass and bare trees to my father's "den". As I crossed the packing shed I had a moment's doubt that he would be there behind the door with his treasures. Then I saw the light under the door and heard him clear his throat. I knocked and went in.

"Well Paul," he said, "we'll have to put a chair in here for you."

"How long have you had all this?"

"A long time." It was all he would tell me. He seemed to feel that in having this room to escape to and books to read he was somehow betraying Mother. I think it eased his mind to have me share the place with him. When he spoke his voice was gruff with affection. I knew without being told that I mustn't tell my mother about the "den". (It was years before I dropped the inverted commas.) As for Andrew—the poison-shed would stay the poison-shed. I had no intention of sharing.

I spent the afternoon reading the titles of my father's books and hunting in them for notes he had written. Were they messages to me? After an hour my mind was fuddled. I looked at him and looked at *Hope*. Like Charlie I nosed around the poison. But always I came back to the books. *Good! True! Alas! Bravo!* And bold mysterious exclamation marks beside lines of poetry like *Oh lyric love, part angel and part bird*. . . .

"Is there nothing there you can read, Paul?" my father asked kindly.

"I'm looking at the parts you've put lines under."

"Would you like me to get you some books?"

I said yes out of a wish to share with him rather than out of a desire to read. My fare until then had been religious stories and the forbidden comics.

"What would you like?"

I could not think.

"Indians?"

"Yes."

"If I let you use this place will you promise not to go near the corner?" He pointed at the poison.

"Yes."

"And will you be careful with the heater? Always have it in the middle of the floor?"

"Yes."

"All right then. I'll get a key made for you."

The thought that I was to have my own key, specially made, kept me in a state of almost passionate contentment for the rest of the afternoon. At half-past four when my father told me to see if my mother wanted any jobs done I ran up to the house whistling. I knew I was special, I knew I was important. I did my mother's jobs from a great height—as a kind of charity. I even picked up my brother John and handed him to her when I saw her begin to get up from her chair. I remember this as the first time I touched him.

On Monday Charlie told me his mother had given him a hiding when he got home. The exercise books were still wet and she could not read some of the bets. To make up for it she had let him go to a Tarzan picture that night. I was unimpressed. I had my father's "den".

I must say something about Andrew. Who is he? Who was he? The things I don't know about him frighten me almost as much as the things I do. He was a large slow-moving child with reddish hair that came from Mother's side of the family. I think of him as being placid, a bit "dim". This can't be right. At school I protected Andrew and came to have the same view of him as the people who wanted to bully him. He wasn't placid, he wasn't "dim". He was closed-in, private. He seemed to be living with his senses dulled. His intelligence was a cut-down adult one. From an early age his responses were ones he had learned. He was a "good" boy. He pleased my mother very much.

Andrew is eighteen months younger than me. Later in our lives he seemed ten years older. But when we were children, away from the house, I treated him as if he were a baby. I "carried" him. I would come across him at school in the lunch hour sitting on a seat by himself. He wanted to play games but didn't know how to join in.

"Come on," I would say, "we're going to play Prisoners' Base." He would join my side, and be the first one caught, and end up sitting in the sun by himself again. At football he would pick up the ball and move a few steps looking for someone to throw it to but always the pack arrived to flatten him before he could get rid of it. He would pick himself up and stare with astonishment at a try being scored in a corner fifty yards away (by me as often as not—I was good). He took injuries in a stoical way but when he was really hurt he cried frankly, without pride. I saved him as often as I could from the bullies attracted by this behaviour. I was in a dozen fights on his account. One day he picked up a flower from the footpath and carried it down the road to drop in the creek. Saving flowers from death on hot pavements was something even I did at times. Mother had taught us plants could feel. But I was always careful not to be seen. Bad luck for the flower if people were about. Andrew had picked up his in front of a bunch of Seddon Tech. boys just off the school train. When I arrived he was howling. They had stuffed the flower down the front of his pants and were lazily whacking his bum with the peaks of their caps. "Pansy Prior," they sang. They were fourteen-year-olds and I was scared. I yelled at Andrew to come on home. I knew though there could be no escape, I was going to get beaten up. I was even calm about it. The Seddon boys didn't want to fight me. I had given them cigarettes at Cascade Park. But they weren't ready to let Andrew go. They kept on beating him and he kept on crying and turning slowly as he looked for a way out of the circle. "Looks like you've got two loony brothers, Prior," they yelled at me.

I hoed in. Their fists came at my face and cracked my teeth. At first I fought with a feeling of elation: this was the way things were, this was what I had to do. But in the end I was blubbing like my brother. The Seddon boys let us go and we went home together, a mess of blood and tears. Andrew still had the flower stuck in his pants.

Outside our house he said, "Don't let Mum see."

"Let's go down the shed," I said. He wanted to avoid upsetting her. She was often sick in these days. I wanted to avoid her blame—I knew it would settle on me, not Andrew. We cleaned ourselves at the tap beside the shed. I had my own key to the "den", hidden between two bricks, but I didn't consider taking him in. I thought of how to get rid of him so I could go in by myself. The window was boarded over and made a good mirror. I wanted to see how badly my teeth were broken. Andrew looked at them and told me two of the front ones had chips broken off.

"Don't let Mum see," he said again.

"How can I stop her?" She looked at our teeth each night before bed.

"She'll be upset."

"It wasn't my fault. What did you have to get in a fight for?" I had a great sense of the injustice of things. I had saved my brother, I had broken teeth and a bruised face, and now I was going to be blamed. I felt like punching him. All he had was a flower in his pants.

"What are you going to do with that?"

He took it out: a sad-looking purple aster. "I'll give it to Mum."

She was sick that night. The flower pleased her. Andrew had his dinner in her bedroom, sitting without complaint on his wounded behind and lifting her spirits with serious opinions. I listened through the door, marvelling at his talent. My father looked at my teeth. Echoing Andrew, he said, "We mustn't let your mother see." When she called me in he answered, "He's doing a job for me, Edith." So I escaped, and the next day my father took me to Auckland, where a dentist ground down the broken edges of my teeth. My mother never found out.

If Andrew was lost at school, about the house he was quick, inventive, jealous. During the winter my father worked around Wadesville as a labour-only carpenter. After John's birth he had built a new room on the house. My mother slept there with John. There was a bed for Andrew too. Often in the middle of the night we were wakened by my father's voice in the new room. There was a regular order of events on these nights. My mother would wake, sick or frightened, and pad bare-footed into Father's room to bring him back to talk with her. He did his duty, yawning, sitting in the hard chair by her bed. It was Andrew she wanted but she never woke him. She knew Father's voice would do that. It woke us both. Andrew would jump out of bed and hurry to the new room. "I'll stay with her, Dad." My father, protesting only a little, would make his way back to bed. Andrew then asked if she would like a cup of tea. He was quick and quiet in the kitchen, and rinsed the cups at the end like a well-trained maid. He put out the light and got into the second bed, but their voices kept on murmuring as I drifted back to sleep. How long they kept it up I don't know. They must have slept some of the time but the first thing I heard when I woke in the morning was the sound of their voices going on and the sound of John in his cot.

It suited me. Everything was being looked after.

Charlie Inverarity said once that he wouldn't mind having "that bear". It was the only time he mentioned our afternoon in my father's den. The afternoon was a kind of watershed in our friendship. I went down into one valley, he into another. At the beginning of the next year we started secondary school. Charlie went to Seddon Tech., I to Mt. Albert Grammar, and though we met in the week-ends, on the train we had to be enemies. Every afternoon after school I went to the den to read or do my homework. My father had bought me *The Last of the Mohicans*. I had not been able to hide from him that I couldn't read it. I think he must have

54

taken advice after that because he bought me books by Rider Haggard and Rafael Sabatini, and Conan Doyle's historical romances. My other reading was handed on to me by Charlie —sixpenny masturbation sheets bought from a Seddon Tech. fifth former called, appropriately, Sticky Leaper. I read about the sporting Mr. Kock who bowled a maiden over, and heroes less restrained. At the same time I was in love with a line of saintly heroines, who came to perfection at last in Agnes Wickfield. In the winter of 1942 I took Dickens at a gulp. The scene itself is Dickensian. The howling wind, the creaking shed, the boy in the lighted room straining his eyes over old books and drinking cups of sweet tea. Outside, the bare grey trees of the orchard, the wet grass and cackling fowl-shed, the quiet house that held Andrew and John and my mother. I became a cave-dweller. My life has changed very little. The outside was there, I lived in it as before: summer, my family, Charlie, school. But I moved back to the den and Father with a feeling of coming home—nothing more was going to be asked of me. I began to read poetry. I was a kind of termite of the printed word working my way through Father's Victorians. Browning, his favourite, became mine too. And his discoveries—once a week he went to the city and visited the second-hand bookshops—also became mine. I read—it astonishes me—*The Light of the World* and *The Light of Asia*, succumbing to a highly-charged religiosity that vanished the moment I stepped outside the den. In the summer of 1944 I read *The Ring and the Book*. I was sick with grief at the murder of Pompilia and would have burned Count Guido at the stake. Outside the den I was having my first real affair with a girl of fifteen called Melva Butler. Charlie said she was the town bike (he was sour at missing his turn) but she had her own sort of morality: she believed in affection, she took on only one boy at a time. She was buck-toothed and I had my father's lumpy nose and coarse pores. Politeness seemed to demand a declaration from me, but after that we didn't pretend to be in love. I learned about menstruation, the dreadful power of semen, how to use French letters (supplied by American servicemen attracted to Wadesville by Dalmation wine). When she tired of me and moved on, I no longer had any use for Sticky Leaper's masturbation sheets. (My nose turned up at them now.) I looked around for another girl.

Andrew was not so lucky. To guide him he had only Mother's lesson that children began in a union of souls. We slept in the same room. One night his voice came out of the dark.

"I think I'm sick."

"What?" I was nearly asleep.

He began to whimper. "There's something coming out of me."

I didn't have to be told what. I threw my handkerchief over. "Don't let it get on your pyjamas." This was all the help I could give. I tried to explain what was happening—tried it blunt and tried it euphemistic—but he answered, "Shut up, shut up," to everything, in a voice that didn't seem to be his. In the end I turned on the light and saw him sitting up in bed with his face mottled pink and white and his eyes closed.

"I've been thinking dirt," he said—not to me. "I promise I won't do it again."

I flipped off the light. A faint whispering started. Listening to the sound of his prayers, I felt a sudden short-lived grief for him. "Andrew, everyone does it." He was beyond reach of advice.

"I promise, God, I promise. I'll never do it again."

He held out for two weeks, then for shorter intervals. I would wake and hear him crying into his pillow.

"For God's sake Andrew, everyone does it. I do it."

"Shut up, shut up."

He tried not to let our mother touch him. He made dawn trips to the creek to get rid of the bits of rag he used. He washed his hands again and again. Sometimes those nights were the ones when he had to make tea for her and sleep in the second bed.

I don't think things became easier for him until she died. She died six months after John, when I was seventeen and Andrew fifteen. John's death comes first. I have put off writing of him—reluctant now to face him as ever. It would be too simple to say that John was conceived as a replacement for me. But some thought like this must have driven my mother. She had married for children, and had seen one of those children move steadily out of the circle of redemption. She had no energy to draw me back, some instinct must have told her the struggle would be hopeless, but she had strength to bring another soul before God. I work in a dim light. As I moved away I understood her less, and if I loved her more deeply, more fiercely, I loved her less often. John was born. My father made some mutterings about God's will, but this was habit. Anger and pain tripped a switch in his mind. He set off along a track already prepared. God for him became an impersonal force, and if His creation was often less than perfect this could be seen as a kind of local accident in the Vast Process of Ongoing. The light is dim for me here too. I followed him only a very short way. His new belief was not evangelistic.

For my mother John's mongolism was more than God's will, it was God's judgement which must not be questioned. I had this from Andrew.

'Why should John be judged?' I asked, 'what had he done?' I was twelve. We were watching our brother in his cot. I too was angry with God. What right had he to do this? To John? To me? Since the Rationalist picnic and the death of the Flynns' cow I had known that people could argue about God and not believe in Him, and that He could make mistakes. I saw that John could be a mistake. He was either that or a punishment. And that meant God was either a fool

57

or wicked—wicked as the devil. For a moment He was more real to me than He had been for years. I hated Him. I told Him to come and strike me now or leave me alone for ever. Nothing happened. Slowly I realized I could hate without fear. He hadn't been able to touch me. And if I could hate Him I could do anything to Him, anything I chose. With a great feeling of power I shrank God down to a dried homunculus. I picked Him up in my fingers and dropped Him out of my life. It was like catching a flea. And that simple expulsion had the power to last. I toyed with my victim for years— God in the grass or in the pile of a carpet, shouting in a tinny voice, "Paul, help me. Help," terrorized by insects. Having Him in this position I forgot Him—no, him—less quickly than I otherwise would have.

I never had a steady feeling about John. I never knew when I saw him moving slackly in his play pen, or became aware of his eyes or mouth or fingers, or heard when I came in at night the snorting adenoidal sounds he made, whether I was going to be overcome with revulsion or fierce protective pity. It made me furious to see Andrew playing with him as though he were a normal child. "For God's sake," I would say, "don't you know he's a loony? Look at his face. Look at the way he slobbers." Andrew would set his face in a look of superiority (both of virtue and understanding) and carry on with the game. My mother's feeling seemed more natural, though I never knew exactly what it was. It was private. She asked no one to share John with her. Andrew chose to and this was both pain and pleasure to her, but at a deeper level it was irrelevant. John was hers, an exchange in the dialogue between her and God. He was what she had been given. Criticism of him was criticism of God. Along with the maternal feelings that made up my mother's love for John went a new painful religious ardour.

But to me (rakehelly, popular, randy Paul) he was a public shame. Sometimes as a kind of test of herself my mother would take him into Wadesville. Even at six years of age he had to be taken in his push-chair. One afternoon they were in the street when the school train arrived at the station. I climbed down to the platform with Andrew but when I saw them I went back into the carriage. Andrew crossed the road, kissed our mother, and put his school-bag on the front of the push-chair. "Where's Paul?" I saw her ask. They looked across the road and saw me sitting in the carriage. Andrew's face went red with rage at what I was doing to her. My mother's expression was one of pity. For the first time in years she seemed to be seeing me. Even John had his slanting eyes on my face. I stared back, sick, accusing, until my mother spoke to Andrew and they went down the street towards home. The train pulled out and I went on to the next station. Sitting in the little orange shed in the the middle of vineyards I made wild plans. I would wait for the train to come back, go to the wharves, work my passage to South America. I would enlist and fight the Japanese. I was sixteen, I could do it. I saw how my death would punish them. Then, calming down, I thought I would simply go into Auckland, get a job and a room, and vanish. But when the train came back I let it go past. I walked along the railway lines to Wadesville and sneaked through the orchard to my father's den. I sat there waiting for him to come and rescue me. After a while I turned on the light and started to do my homework. My father came down after dark. I knew from the noise of his boots in the packing shed that he was angry with me. I wanted to run again. Even the den wasn't safe.

"You've got no consideration, Paul. Your brother is ill, your mother's frantic. And on top of this you don't come home. It's very thoughtless of you."

I asked what was wrong.

"Your brother's having convulsions. They think he's dying."

"Andrew?" I said, stupified.

"John."

I remember thinking, Good. Good that he was dying, good that it wasn't Andrew. Then I started to cry. My father put his hand on my shoulder.

"It's all right, Paul. We've always expected it, haven't we?"

"Yes," I said.

"Do you want to come up now?"

"I'll stay here."

My father went back to the house. Later he brought me some bread and a cold chop. I sat in the den eating, drinking tea. I began to feel safe, I began to feel happy. It became a kind of picnic.

At about ten o'clock my father came down again to tell me John was dead.

My mother's death, by far the more important event for me then, seems now only a coda. She died of a kidney disease that had begun to trouble her shortly after John was born. In the last months of her life she could not leave her bed. My father hired a woman to nurse her and do the housework. This woman, Mrs. Philips, cooked small delicate meals for my mother ("What we've got to do is tempt the poor lamb") and mountains of greens and potatoes for us. The only instruction mother gave was, "Make sure they get enough to eat." Out of duty she made this foray into the world, and did not know how out of character she sounded. I've never found out where she was the rest of the time. Andrew probably knows.

She went into a coma on the day the Pacific war ended. Church bells were ringing and the fire siren sounding when the ambulance arrived to take her to hospital. She died the next day.

My father started going to the Unitarian Church. Andrew stayed a Presbyterian. Liking words more than meanings, I called myself an agnostic.

## May 13–16, 1969

When I offered Fernie breakfast he said he was going off duty
soon and would have something at home. I couldn't decide
whether he didn't want to eat with me or be caught eating
with me. While I had my egg and toast he sat at the table
reading the morning paper.

"Any news?"

"No." He accepted a cup of coffee. Fernie reminded me of
boys I had taught—the sort who became head prefect or
captain of the school. There was the same pause in behaviour: uncertainty hidden behind a clear eye while the mind
hung over the abyss of decision: then a retreat to the rules. I
wondered how often he had looked at me during the night to
make sure I wasn't slashing my wrists or dressing for a break
to the Waitakeres.

"What's going to happen this morning?"

"Nothing that I know of."

"Am I going to be arrested?"

"I couldn't say. You'd better ask Inspector Farnon."

"When will he be coming?"

"When he's finished at the park."

It went on like this until half-past eight. I told Fernie I'd
recommend him highly and he gave a regulation smile. We
were both beginning to wonder why he hadn't been relieved.

I read the newspaper and saw the finger pointing at me. It
was neatly done. For the first time I thought of looking for
help. My lawyer was an old Unitarian friend of my father's. I

hadn't needed him for years and I knew he'd be bewildered by this sort of case. Andrew had a lawyer who'd been in his class at Mt. Albert Grammar. I saw then that Andrew was exactly what I needed—a dose of his cold neat voice, a dose of common sense.

I asked Fernie if I could use the phone. He consulted behind his eyes.

"All right."

I rang Andrew's number. His wife answered. "Paul? I was going to ring you. I've just read the paper."

Penny was not what I needed. Her passion for "deciding what should be done" led her unfailingly to moral precepts, heartily pronounced—"We must buck up, we must try harder." I said I would ring the factory and I hung up. I had never phoned Andrew at work before and I had to look for his number in the book. When I got through his secretary told me he was in the wood-turning shop. She said she would ask him to ring me when he came back.

Fernie had listened without seeming to. "What do you want your brother for?"

"To get the name of a lawyer." I saw how everything I did could count against me, and I asked Fernie if he would do his waiting outside. I said I was tired of having people lounging around my house.

He smiled. "Not long now, Mr. Prior."

I went to the bathroom and had a shave. The face in the mirror looked like a murderer's. It had muddy brown eyes with sore lids; a doughy nose; girlish lips that looked as though they'd been sucking plums. Celia couldn't have liked me. Had I found out? Had I killed her? I searched for a gap in my life and a fear that I was on the point of finding it nearly made me cry out. Fernie came to the door.

"Bugger off," I said. He smiled and went away.

I shaved. I grew calmer. There was no gap in my life. Somebody else had killed her. Farnon would find out. And

Celia *had* liked me. Poor Celia, poor dear girl. It's all over now, I told her. With approval, I felt my eyes fill with tears. Then, "Phony bastard," I said. Why hadn't she seen through me? Look at that arty hair curling round the ears. I slashed at one of my sideburns and took it off with two blows of the razor. Then I started to laugh. Childish, it was childish. Look at me, all lopsided. I told myself I should stay like that, as penance, like a Catholic. But I took the other sideburn off, trimmed them up, and put some after-shave lotion on my face. I went back to the den and told Fernie I was going to make another pot of coffee.

A phone call came for him at half-past nine.

"I've got to leave now. The Inspector wants you to stay here. He's coming to see you later on."

"What's happening?"

"I've no idea."

"He must have found out it wasn't me."

I went outside and watched Fernie walk away. They must be busy, I realized, if they didn't have a car to send for him. It was a cold windy day and I thought what a bleak start it was to the term holidays. Then I thought of Celia lying in a morgue while a rubber-gloved expert made an inventory of her parts. Thorax, lungs, liver. Where was her murderer? Who was he? Once I'd thought of a Maori face when I tried to picture criminals. Later it changed to pakeha—a relief to me. Neither would come that morning. I tried the stereotype: sex-fiend—mousy, wearing pebble glasses. The only face I could find was my own. I went inside and started to tidy the house. I threw the herb leaves into the fire-place and put *The First Circle* in the bookcase. Then because I was close to my chair I sat down. I remembered a girl in a London pub who had told me I looked like Jack the Ripper. No, I thought, it wasn't me. Farnon knows. It was some bloody thug, some Maori. They probably had him by now. But I had to find out. The only person I could think of to ring was Jim Beavis.

63

Margaret Beavis answered the phone. I heard a quick indrawn breath as she recognized my voice.

"Jim's down at Cascade Park. He's helping the police."

I thought "helping the police in their investigations". But at the same time Margaret's voice was running on. "They wanted local residents to help search the scrub. Jim volunteered. He's one of the ones doing the edge of the creek."

"Have they found anything?"

"I don't know. I don't think I should talk any more, Paul."

"Why not?"

"I don't think people should talk——"

"You mean because I'm a suspect?"

"No——"

"Your bloody husband's more likely to have done it than me." I hung up. I was trembling. I got a glass from the kitchen and poured myself a whisky. Then I thought it would look bad to Farnon if I had whisky on my breath when he came. I took the drink to my chair. To hell with him, I thought, to hell with Farnon. And to hell with Margaret Beavis, pin-headed bitch. (She's a kind, sensible woman.) I wanted to be left alone. I wanted to think about Celia.

It was eleven o'clock before Farnon arrived. I went to the door to let him in. Glover was opening the garage. "What's he looking for?" I asked.

"Just checking one or two things, Mr. Prior."

Farnon was relaxed this morning. He asked me if I'd had a good night. Glover came in. He gave a quick nod to Farnon.

"All right, Mr. Prior. It seems you're off the hook."

I should have been angry. Instead I was grateful, as though he'd made me a gift. I said, "Thank you."

He sat down. "You might be able to help us." Glover took out his flip-pad. "Whoever did it we'll get him. That's certain now. We've got enough to go on. But you might be able to cut the thing short."

I saw why he was relaxed. Last night he'd thought he had

his man, he was keyed up for the last step. This morning he was back to routine work.

"How did you decide it wasn't me?"

"Her finger-prints weren't in the car. That was the first thing. Then we found another boy who'd been at the park. . . . Why didn't you tell us Celia borrowed some books yesterday?"

"I didn't think."

"What were they?"

"*Leaves of Grass*, by Walt Whitman."

"Yes."

"That's poetry."

"The other one?"

"James Hogg. *Memoirs and Confessions of a Justified Sinner*."

Glover's mouth went straight as he wrote it down.

"It's about religion. Calvinism." I was more defensive than yesterday: I wanted to please them.

Farnon showed no emotion. He went on before Glover had finished writing. "There was a car there with the door open. The books were lying on the ground. The boy put them back inside and he saw your name in one of them. He goes to your school. But he says the car wasn't yours because it didn't have a scratch along the left side."

I saw why Glover had gone into the garage. "I've been meaning to have it painted," I said.

"The boy put the books on the front seat. We think he's lucky the murderer didn't come back."

"Yes."

"Did Celia know any fair-haired men?"

"I don't know."

"We found someone who might have seen him. A woman who drove up Farm Road yesterday afternoon. She passed Celia going into the gully. She also saw you going back inside."

"I don't remember——"

"She noticed a small blue car—blue or green—parked off the road on the other side of the gully. There was a man standing beside it. All she can say is she thinks he had fair hair."

"He must have watched us."

"We had a look at the place this morning. You can see your house and the gate and the whole stretch of road. Our guess is he watched her all the way. But we don't think she would have got in the car unless she knew him."

"Or unless she'd had too much sherry," Glover said.

Farnon smiled slightly. "Bob's not too happy with your part in this. Nor am I, to tell the truth."

"It was only a small glass." I wanted nothing now except that they would trust me—I wanted to help. I was guilty about the sherry. (Recognizing guilt has always been a form of expiation with me—quick and almost painless. But Farnon and Glover weren't going to let me use the trick.)

Farnon said, "It's a question of how much her judgement was impaired. She wasn't the sort of girl to get in a car with anyone?"

"No."

"Unless she was more careless than usual?"

"She wasn't. It was half an inch. A child could have drunk it."

"A child did," Glover said.

"All right, Bob. We're going to believe you, Mr. Prior, but I think I should warn you now, this business of the sherry's going to come up. You can probably make it easier for yourself by helping all you can."

"What do you want me to do?"

"You might be able to give us a short-cut. You knew her better than anyone outside the family. She talked to you about herself. What you do is, you write down the name of every man she ever mentioned. If you can't remember names you write down descriptions. If you don't know that you write down what she said. Okay?"

"Yes."

"Have you got a pen and paper?"

I fetched them and sat down again. I thought. There weren't any names. "She liked ugly men."

"Enough of the jokes, Mr. Prior."

"I'm not joking. That's what she said. There's a chap who works in one of the butcher shops. She said he was fabulous —the ugliest man in Wadesville."

Glover was looking mutinous, and Farnon said shortly, "All right. Write it down."

I wrote. "There was a student she met at a National Orchestra concert. She had a cup of coffee with him and he wanted to take her out."

"Did she go?"

"No. She said he had bad breath."

"What was his name?"

"She called him Bertie Wooster. Look, don't get mad at me. . . ."

In the end I had three names and two descriptions. I handed the paper to Farnon. He looked at it sourly.

"You're a great help, Mr. Prior."

I offered to make them a cup of tea. Farnon said no and jerked his head at Glover. In the hall he said, "I'll be back to see you. I've got a feeling about you. You've got something for me, even though you mightn't know what it is." I told him I was anxious to help.

"Have you had a report from the pathologist?"

I was on the porch by then and he was half-way down the path. He looked back at me. For a moment I thought he wasn't going to answer. Then he said, "We've got some preliminary stuff. You're sure you want to hear it?"

"Yes."

"She wasn't raped. He didn't touch her that way."

"Thank God."

"You think so, Mr. Prior? She was half scalped. He tried to rip her hair out." He held up his thumbs. "Her throat was crushed."

"All right." I turned away.

"And before he strangled her he tried to kick her inside out."

"All right."

"You still want to thank God?"

I went inside and closed the door. In the den I saw the pad and pen I had used lying on the table by my chair. I picked them up and wrote, *Celia. Celia Inverarity. Her throat was crushed. I'm sorry*, I wrote, *I'm sorry. Dear girl.* I looked at the paper for a while, then screwed it up and burnt it in the fireplace.

I went to the room where I kept school materials and took the top book from the pile of 3 Professional English project books. It belonged to a boy called Peter Adderley. I ripped the used pages out—I would not be going back to Wadesville College—and carried the book to the den. I fetched scissors and paste, cut the news item on Celia's murder from the *Express*, and pasted it over the first few pages. I sat down and thought. After a while I wrote, *Celia was eleven the first time I saw her. She was wearing a blue dress and white socks and sandals. Her hair was done in the tightest pigtails I had ever seen. We were in her father's shop. I had just come back from Europe and had not seen Wadesville for fourteen years. It was no longer the town I was born in. Everything was changed and I felt lost. I remembered the way it was in the thirties. . . .*

It did not seem strange to me that I had begun so soon to write about myself. I would come back to Celia. But I had to find a shape. Shape might be understanding.

I had covered five or six pages when the phone rang. I went into the hall, thinking it must be Farnon.

Andrew said, "Paul? You wanted me?"

68

I felt something between a sinking of the heart and the shock of accident. I tried to get rid of him and back to my writing.

"It's all right now. Thanks for ringing."

"Just a minute. What's going on? Penny's been on the phone trying to tell me something about a girl who's been killed."

"There was a murder. A girl I knew. She was strangled at Cascade Park. The police thought I might have done it."

There was a silence.

"You? That's absurd."

"I know it's absurd. But I was the last one to see her. I wanted the name of your lawyer."

"Lester Bowman. Watters and Bowman."

"It's all right. I don't need him now. They've got a suspect."

"Who?"

"A man with fair hair, in a Mini like mine, blue or green. A woman saw him and some kids saw the car."

Another silence, longer. "Andrew?" I said.

"Sorry. My secretary wanted me. Stupid woman." Stupid, for him, was a kind of swear word. "This girl. Penny said her name was Inverarity. Does that mean she was Charlie's daughter?"

"That's right."

"How's he taking it?" Andrew had it fixed in his mind that Charlie and I were still friends. I had given up trying to explain.

"I haven't seen him."

"The police think they've got someone, do they?"

"A fair-haired man. That's all they know."

"It lets you out."

We went on like this for a while, then he asked me to dinner during the week. I said I would call Penny and let her know. Back at my writing, I found I couldn't go on. The neat little groove Andrew had run in since our mother's death produced

69

in me even now an impatience that was close to anger. For God's sake man, I wanted to say, shake yourself, break out, do something. How, I wondered, had he managed to marry Penny—and father a child?

I made some lunch and started again. After a while I found my way back to my place. I wrote through the afternoon. A little after five I drove to the "Golden Mile" and bought some vegetables and meat. Outside a dairy the *Telegraph* billboard said: *Wadesville Girl Slain. Murder Hunt.* I bought a copy and drove home.

There was a picture of Celia on the front page. She was in school uniform. Another picture showed Farnon briefing his men at Cascade Park. In the front row of the locals was Jim Beavis, in Fair Isle sweater and tramping boots. The search had turned up nothing. I read about the fair-haired man, the car, the missing copies of *Leaves of Grass* and *Memoirs and Confessions of a Justified Sinner* with the name Paul Prior in them. There would be a run on libraries, and some disappointed borrowers. But I felt a little sick—I was lucky to have got out of the shopping area without being recognized. I wondered if Farnon would tell the reporters I'd given Celia sherry.

There was nothing in the paper about Charlie and Joyce.

After dinner I settled down to write again. I had come to my meeting with Celia, and was working with a feeling of unease and excitement; conscious both of controlling and of being controlled. I was taken at moments by a simple almost superstitious dread: at the end of this, completing it, must be the murderer. I was aware too of no longer being safe in my den. All my life I had kept people out. For women, other acquaintance, I had learned the trick of switching on an ordinary room. And for the den I had shaped a Celia who was not a real one. Now, here, was the real one. I finished Peter Adderley's book and started on another.

Towards nine o'clock something thumped on the front

wall of the house and rattled across the porch. Part of my unease was a sense of being in danger from Wadesville. This was the first attack.

I turned out the light and listened. There was a sudden chatter of stones on the roof. One of my bedroom windows shattered. A cheer came from the road. I heard it with relief. Children. This was something I could handle. I opened the front door and went on to the porch. Another cheer went up. My schoolteacher's ear caught the uncertainty in it. "Go home," I called out. There were a dozen of them: shadowy figures in the diluted light of the street-lamp by the hollow.

"Pansy Prior," sang one of the boys. (Tonight they would not call me "Pepsi".)

"Go home before you get yourselves in trouble."

"What did you do to Celia, Pansy?"

"Yeah, yeah?"

"Windy Prior. Pansy Prior."

"Hey Windy, who's next on your list? Is it Barbara Carson?"

"Pauline Jones?"

"How about Pauline? She's got big tits."

They were naming sixth-form girls. I had recognized the leaders by now and I called them by name. "Go on, Spencer. Take them away. Mason. You're not stupid enough to think you can get away with a thing like this."

"Yah, Pansy Prior, Jack the Ripper."

"If you're not gone in two minutes I'll call the police."

"They'll arrest you, not us."

"Get out."

"Not before we've cut your balls off, Pansy."

This brought shrieks of laughter. I turned from the edge of the porch towards the door. At once stones began to thud around me. One hit the back of my knee. A cheer went up as I hobbled to the door. Another cracked into the side of my head. I thought I was going to black out. I managed to get

71

inside and slam the door. Blood trickled down my cheek. There was blood in the cheering too. They'd burn my house, they'd butcher me. But I had forgotten my threat. They must have thought I was phoning for the police. They used their stones up quickly and rode off shrieking into the hollow and up the hill towards town.

I bathed my scalp and went to bed. I lay awake sweating and shivering. The children had had their turn. What would the adults do?

In the morning I cleaned up the mess. Every window in the front of the house was broken. I nailed sacks over them, picked up the glass inside, and swept the porch. It was covered with river-bed pebbles taken, I guessed, from the Japanese garden outside the Borough Council offices. The exercise made me calmer. I decided not to lay a complaint. In a few days, when I had finished my writing, I would leave Wadesville for good.

I wrote all that day and late into the night. Nobody came near me. I learned from the radio news that no arrest had been made. The police were following several leads. In bed, I went to sleep quickly. The noise of a car woke me at three o'clock. I heard the sound of my gate being opened. I lay stiff with dread. I tried to stop the noise of my heart and the faint noises my stiffened body drew from the bed. Footsteps sounded on the gravel path. I had no thought of the Wadesville vigilantes. This was the murderer coming for me. The footsteps came on to the porch. Rubbery. Male. There was a heavy thump. And then—I nearly cried out with relief— noise on the gravel again; the gate; the car.

I kept my blood still. The old house made creaking sounds. A light wind puffed the sacks at the windows. At ten past three I got up and turned on the lights. I fetched the small tomahawk from the hearth in my den and opened the front door. The light made a track across the porch and into the garden. In the centre of it lay a small pile of books and a record.

Charlie had paid a visit.

I wasn't surprised; instead I was angry. It pleased me that he was up in the night. It pleased me that he was grieving. And I was contemptuous that this was the best he could do— dump my presents to Celia back on my porch. I took them into the den. The books carried cautious inscriptions: *To Celia Inverarity from Paul Prior*. I got my pen. In the first two, Yeats's *Collected Poems* and *Persuasion*, I wrote: *With love*. But when I came to the third, *The New Zealand Sea Shore*, I saw the absurdity of what I was doing. I sat in my chair shivering. The sacks puffed in and out, as though the house were breathing. With a small tinkle a piece of glass fell on the window ledge. In the shadows *Hope* sat demurely on the world with her finger poised at the string of her lyre. After a while I put the record on the player and sat back to listen. It was a gesture at once sentimental and defiant, but both emotions were in a low key. The delicate formal music soothed me further. It was Pergolasi's *Concerto in G for flute and strings*. I wondered that a girl so fiery as Celia had had a taste for this sort of music. It came to me that in thinking of her without grief or horror, and playing this concerto to which some gentle part of her had responded, I was conducting a service for her, in place of the one I would not be able to go to.

I played the recording several times. When I heard the milkman at the gate I went to bed; and later went to sleep, when light began to enter the room and the sacks hung without moving in the stillness of dawn.

In the afternoon I had a visit from Farnon. He was looking tired. His nose seemed softer, less like a beak. I offered him a cup of tea. He asked me about the cut on my head and the broken windows. I told him what had happened, but he showed little interest.

"Have you any idea how many blue and green Minis there are in Auckland?"

The names I had given him had been "checked out". The

fair-haired men in the western suburbs, and dark-haired too, with cars of the right sort had alibis. He had come for another list: the names of all my friends. He still felt there was a clue in me.

"Why did he stop on the hill, the only place where he could see your house?"

I wrote down the names of half a dozen people, a little disturbed that I should feel pleasure, however ill-defined, in bringing misfortune to my acquaintance (friends was Farnon's term).

He read the list and said, "You don't seem to be the most popular man in the world. These are all people who know where you live?"

"Yes."

"What about your brother?"

"He's got a black Rover." I saw no reason to have Andrew bothered.

"All right," said Farnon grumpily. He thanked me for the tea and went away.

Late in the afternoon I went to New Lynn to buy provisions. I told myself it was distaste for Wadesville that made me reluctant to enter it again. I bought enough to last several days. On the way home I stopped and looked at my house from the place where the murderer had waited. The roof was cherry red in an afterglow from the setting sun. The walls had a faint pink glow and the paddocks around were emerald green, dotted with rust-red cattle. (I use my mother's colour-chart.) In this defining light I could almost make out the leaves on the shrubs beside the path. I saw the brown rectangles of the sacks over the windows, and white pebbles on the veranda roof. Closer to me, in the hollow, was the ruin of the old shack where Celia had picked leaves of herb. I saw how she had walked from my house in plain view, gone out of sight behind scrub—on that afternoon it must have had this same pinkish glow—and come out again in her Quaker mini-

74

frock and Crusader's cap of shining hair only twenty yards away. What had happened then? Had his motive been simply destruction of beauty? of innocence? Had he been simply an unhappy man, or sick; no monster, no evil being? And the happy girl an affront? As simple as that? I could understand his impulse to kill. But not the turning of it to action. That was monstrous, that was evil. I saw it as an amoebic reaching out, ingesting; the excreting of a corpse sucked dry. What sort of life had he taken from hers? How had he grown? What was the gain?

I turned myself from this sort of indulgence. But I had seen that the killing might have taken place here, not at Cascade Park. If I had waited on my veranda I might have heard it. I got into my car and drove to the edge of the road. This brought the valley into sight. When I was at school I had a teacher who liked to call Wadesville "the garden of Auckland". Most of the orchards and vineyards are rated out now. I saw their pattern further up the valley. In their place are factories, warehouses, schools, playing fields; and houses, battalion after battalion, drawn up neatly along the sealed streets: brick, tile, weather-board, coloured iron. The creeks seem to have shrunk. The trees have been shaved from their banks. Concrete bridges stand in place of the wooden ones. The largest patch of water I could see was the pool where Charlie and I had launched our canoes. It was pinkish grey. For a moment I thought it was catching some final glow from the sky, then I realized a coloured waste from one of the factories had been fed into it. Just beyond, where Prior's orchard had been, are the huge fibrolite storage sheds of the Apple and Pear Marketing Board.

I turned back to my rural corner. It had survived by a quirk of the commercial spirit. The owner of those paddocks calmly fattened his dozen Herefords, watching the price of land go up. I could guess from his smile that sub-division was not far away. And my acre, with its wild back garden and pair of elderly ewes? I would sell too. Wadesville was out of my system.

But I was not out of Wadesville's system. Three cars came that night. Two pairs of feet crunched the gravel.

"Mr. Prior?" said the older man. He was almost six and a half feet tall, with thin shoulders and a belly that protruded suddenly, like a growth. I recognized him as Len Coope, the owner of a failing coffee shop called The Chicken Coope.

"Yes?" I said.

"We're from the Wadesville Action Committee. We're holding a meeting at Cascade Park."

"What's the Wadesville Action Committee?"

"We'd like you to come."

"I don't want to come. What is this committee?"

"We'd like you to come, Mr. Prior."

The younger man (my dentist, Wilson) was more direct. "We're telling you to come," he said. He took my arm and tried to pull me on to the veranda. I shook myself free.

"Look," I protested. At the same time I tried to close the door. Len Coope thrust it open with his shoulder. His eyes began to pop. "Enough mucking about," he cried. He grabbed a handful of my sleeve and jerked me on to the veranda. Wilson took my other arm and they started to frog-march me to the cars.

"All right," I yelled, "just let me change my slippers."

"Ha!" Wilson said.

"Left right, left right," Len Coope said.

They put me in the back seat of a car and got in on either side. In convoy we drove to Cascade Park. Lynching, I thought, they're going to lynch me. In this I was simply rising to the occasion. Some sort of humiliation was more likely. I was less frightened than during Charlie's visit. Only a week ago one of these men had breathed peppermint down my throat.

"What's going to happen?" I said in a voice whose steadiness pleased me.

There were a dozen cars at the park, lined up with their

76

lights on facing the patch of scrub where Celia's body had been found. Of the group of men in the space the only one I recognized was Lionel Pinckney, the mayor. He seemed to be making a speech. Wilson got out of the car and Coope prodded me to follow.

"I warn you again," came Pinckney's voice, "if you carry on with this you'll be breaking the law. It's on the agenda for the next council meeting. We'll discuss it then and action will be taken. Will be. That's a promise. But this sort of thing is no solution. It's—undemocratic."

A man at the back of the group gave a single loud guffaw. The others made no sound. As Wilson and his group brought me forward the man facing Pinckney turned his shoulder to him. "The time for talking's over." He beckoned Wilson. "Bring him here."

This man was Max Hobhouse, accountant at my bank. His resentment that a schoolteacher should have a private income had grown over the years into a kind of moral disgust. I had taken to writing letters to the Wadesville *Gazette*. They were prompted partly by conscience, but chiefly, I see now, they emphasized my isolation, which I looked on as a kind of royal state. From the comfort of my den I loosed my shots at Wadesville, like the Sultan who amused himself by picking off his subjects from a turret on his palace walls. Hobhouse replied shot for shot. He wrote short bullet-shaped sentences. In the town's eyes he slew me again and again. My response was Phoenix-like and Protean. The latter angered him more. I thought now as Wilson led me to him through the car-lights how fitting it was that he should be my tormentor. Barbered, glittering, he faced me. I smiled. I almost said, "So Hobhouse, we meet again." A second later I was quivering with terror. Several of the men had cans of petrol at their feet: they were going to burn me. Hobhouse was quick, he had my thought by the time I looked back at him from the cans. I saw him almost taste my fear. There was, at once, a

77

look of intense pleasure in his eyes, and a hunger for more.

"I've got a witness," I cried, and I waved my hand at Pinckney. But then I had control. Common sense told me what was possible. Not burning, not in Wadesville. Not even humiliation—shaved head or nugget on the balls. Hobhouse might try. The others were mustered Rotarians, angry Bowling Club men. Ignoring them, ignoring Pinckney, who had walked away from my claim on him, I said, "All right, Max. Get on with the charade, whatever it is."

He watched me for a few seconds, in a kind of querulous disappointment, trying to see how I'd got away. "Get the petrol," he said loudly. I smiled at him. He turned and went to his car and came back with a can and an armful of rags.

"You were supposed to be 'a friend' of the girl. So we thought you'd like to be present. Don't try and leave till we tell you."

He turned to the men. It was happening quicker than he wanted. "All right, boys. Let's get started." As a signal he dropped his rags on the ground and splashed petrol on them. The other men moved off to the edge of the scrub and took positions at intervals along it. They began to soak rags and push them between manuka trunks and into thickets of bracken. The scrub patch faced them like a cornered animal. I was moved by its plight; by its silent, still acceptance. But the men too were quiet, dignified. I began to be on their side as I watched. It seemed like a rite in some primitive religion. It was communal, an action of force, I felt a stirring in my blood. The scrub appeared momentarily as the amoebic creature that had broken Celia. Hobhouse had gone along the path to the clearing where the boys had found her body. As leader he had taken the heart-thrust for himself. When I caught myself thinking this I came to my senses. I put a sneer on my face.

"What good do they think this will do?" I said to Pinckney.

He was ten feet away, and moved two more.

"Taking it out on a patch of scrub. It's childish."

Again he moved.

"I was brought here against my will," I said.

"That's no business of mine."

I listened to the voices of the men quietly giving instructions. The only other noise came from the waterfalls a hundred yards away. On the hill beyond the creek I could see people watching from lighted windows. Why hadn't they watched like this on Sunday afternoon? I felt I had to talk to someone and I said to Pinckney, "Surely some of those people must have seen the murder."

"The police have made inquiries," he answered stiffly. He went to sit in his car.

I walked towards the swimming hole. Men were working on the flank of scrub that curved towards the creek. The tent-shaped frame that had held the swings rose out of knee-high bracken. Beyond it were the changing sheds, stripped of most of their corrugated iron. One wall of the Ladies hung out at an angle of forty-five degrees. Nobody swam at the Cascades any more. It was polluted. The sheds would go in the fire. I wondered if Hobhouse had realized that. I turned back. A faint glow came from the middle of the scrub. I saw men along the rim strike matches and throw them towards the hidden rags. Suddenly a dozen fires were burning. Hobhouse came running into the open. He turned twenty yards from the scrub and stood hands on hips to watch it. Some of the fires burned slowly. The scrub was damp. Others suddenly flared and rushed. A light cold wind was blowing. It carried the larger fires into the heart as Hobhouse's one moved towards the creek. Soon the whole rim was alight. Heavy wet-looking smoke rolled up and vanished into the dark. At the cars the faces of the men were red from the light. Hobhouse's eyes glowed like embers. Ginger hairs stood out in his black moustache. He had come to stand at my side. From time to time he shouted orders. Several men took sacks down to the swimming hole and brought them back wet to beat out flames that might come through the grass towards the cars. But the wind was holding the main fire in place. The only danger was to a house by the park entrance. A man was hosing its walls.

Hobhouse glanced at me from time to time. He didn't need to say anything. I stood feeling miserable, my face hot and my back cold. Soon, far away, I heard a fire siren, and later the sound of an approaching engine.

"All right, men," Hobhouse yelled. "We've done what we had to do." They were "boys" no longer, but I hadn't the spirit to comment. The Wadesville Action Committee left, without offering me a ride home. I was impressed by the discipline that enabled them to leave a fire as spectacular as this. Down by the creek flames were leaping twenty feet into the air. From the damper parts of the scrub smoke coiled up as thick as cream. Children on bicycles rode back and forth, screeching like berserk Redskins. Others with torches of twisted newspaper were starting new fires in the bracken. The engine stopped at the park gates and two firemen appeared, uncoiling a hose. Soon a jet of water arched into the flames. It made no difference that I could see. The firemen extended their hose and saved the changing sheds. For this they were booed. My slippers were soaked, I shook with cold, but I stayed until the flames of the main fire started to die down. There was an extravagance in these events that led me to see my discomfort as a kind of offering to Celia. As I went out the gates I passed Jim and Margaret Beavis strolling down to see what was left of the fire. They smiled at me with embarrassment. Further on, Hobhouse was sitting in his car. He lit a cigarette so I would see his face. I walked across the edge of our "quiet" suburb (it's still a town to me) and started along Farm Road. I was half-way along when a car came up behind me. The driver leaned across and opened the door. "Jump in." It was Farnon.

I got in gratefully. (So much for my offering.) He started again and drove slowly. "All right?" he asked.

"Yes."

"I heard you were down there. What happened?"

I told him.

"You could bring a charge."

"What's the point?"

"I'll have something to say to them." He was angry on behalf of "the scene of the crime". Now that I thought of it, I was glad it was burned. We started down towards the hollow.

"Have you thought she might have been killed there?" I nodded at the place where the woman had seen the Mini.

"What makes you think that?"

I told him I had stopped there earlier. "If he was insane, a girl coming up like Celia, looking——" I began to flounder —"happy—beautiful—it could have been an impulse—a sudden attack. . . ."

"We had a good look. There's nothing there. No marks. Not a thing." He was interested though. When we stopped at my gate he turned on the inside light. "I still think you can come up with something. Keep going over it, will you? Everything you've ever known about the girl. Everything she's ever said."

"Yes." I asked about the list I had made.

"We're going through it. But I don't expect anything from that."

"What about cars?"

He smiled. "There's two men we've got with the right sort of car and no alibi. One's a bloke who quarrelled with his wife and just went out and drove. He's got black hair. The other one's a bald homosexual."

"Well——"

"It's not him. I know where he was."

"What do you do then?"

"We go wider. If that doesn't work we start again."

"You'll get him."

"That's right. But I'd rather do it quickly."

I promised to keep thinking, and he let me out and drove away.

The next morning Andrew's wife rang and asked me to dinner. I said yes more eagerly than I would ever have thought possible. After I had put the phone down I got in my car and drove to Waikumete. I parked behind pine trees at the highest point of the road along the back of the reserve. Between two trunks I looked across the acres of white headstones and crosses to the crematorium. Away to the right, among trees, stood the old brick building where my father had been cremated more than twenty years before. I wished they were taking Celia there.

I had been waiting only ten minutes when the procession arrived. I counted the first twenty cars, then gave up. There must have been more than a hundred. An almost invisible smoke began to rise from the chimney as men in dark suits lifted the coffin from the hearse and carried it into the chapel through an avenue of children in Wadesville College uniforms. I waited a long time. Charlie had no religion, but Joyce Poole, I remembered, had been Church of England, and probably was again for this occasion. After twenty minutes the smoke from the chimney suddenly darkened. I got in my car and drove away. Like Farnon's man who had quarrelled with his wife I simply kept going. I went through Riverhead, Silverdale, and found myself after midday at Orewa. I walked on the beach for an hour. A cold wind was blowing off the sea. A man and a girl in black rubber suits were surfing where the waves ran in towards the river mouth. The man was expert; patient with the girl, who kept falling off.

At one o'clock I had a cup of coffee in a milk bar. I started to drive south towards Takapuna. Once I stopped myself from turning the car round and chasing a green Mini. Farnon's job. There were thousands of green Minis.

As I drove past the old church at Albany I wondered what Charlie and Joyce were going to do with Celia's ashes.

## 1945–1949

My father grew Cox's Orange and Gravenstein apples and
Bon Chretien pears. For household use we had plum, lemon,
grapefruit, peach and nectarine trees and a small grove of
tree tomatoes (tamarillos today). My mother made jam and
marmalade and bottled the tree tomatoes and nectarines.
Her fowls kept us supplied with eggs whose yolks had a
colour seldom seen in these days of battery production. They
sometimes layed in the orchard. Andrew and I would scout
through the grass and come back with our shirts full of eggs
which Mother would test for freshness in a pan of water.
After her death Father wanted to sell the fowls but Andrew
begged to look after them himself. He began to sell eggs
round the neighbourhood. The cow died and as the Flynns
had left Wadesville we decided to get our milk from the milkman. I was happy to be relieved of the job of milking. I was
no farmer, not really even a countryman. As Wadesville
turned towards light industry in the years after the war I
came to think of the orchard as no more than a suitably
picturesque setting for my love affairs.

In spite of this I always seemed to be working in it. My
father was an old man and he gave himself up more and more
to the pleasures of talk with his Unitarian cronies (his term).
We had reached an agreement that he would pay my way
through university if I would work holidays in the orchard.
For spending money he let me set up a week-end stall at the

side of the road. I sold not only apples and pears but plums in season, tree tomatoes, nectarines and peaches, grapefruit, lemons, and eggs for Andrew (Saturdays only) on a small commission. A number of my girl-friends served in the stall but I made it clear that I couldn't afford to pay them. One season I manoeuvred two of them in. While they competed there I swotted, i.e. read George Eliot, down by the creek.

Mrs. Philips who had nursed mother came in the afternoons to clean the house and cook for us. She still served mountains of mashed potatoes and curly kale, and either lambs fry baked into boards or boiled neck of mutton chops. I started to eat in Auckland but this upset Father. So I learned to cook. Mrs. Philips was demoted to floor-scrubber etc. Because it was summer I started with a cabbage salad. Andrew grumbled about my "arty ideas". My father found raw cabbage hard on his teeth. I gave them potato salad the next night, using olive oil bought from the chemist. I began to buy recipe books. The kitchen became a kind of laboratory where I mixed fantastic brews. It wasn't easy in those days of shortages; but slowly I acquired the skill that as much as any other has made it possible for me to live without a woman. My father began to enjoy his food. He had always been a rough and ready eater. Now he made a ritual of tasting. He liked foreign foods best: spaghetti, chow mein, Indian curries. They allowed him to orate on national character. He was always at his most xenophilic when I served the local red wine. The Dalmatians were wonderful people, he said, we should bring more of them in—and Russians, Italians, Greeks, Chinese. My trouble came from Andrew.

"What have we got tonight?" he would ask when he came in from his work at the bank.

"Hawaian steak."

"Any garlic in that?"

"I left it off your bit."

He would reject a meal out of hand at the first sniff of garlic

84

or taste of any unusual spice. The appearance of spaghetti made him feel sick, unless it was the sort that came out of tins. And Chinese food ("raw vegetables"), rice ("supposed to be in puddings"), oil ("dago stuff"), he refused to accept as civilized. He grumbled at the wine my father and I drank. Second glasses made him frown terribly, and if I reached out to pour a third he would lock himself in his room.

Andrew was guardian of all things that had been our mother's, from ideas down to lace handkerchiefs. Her preserved fruit was of the middle order of relics. He doled it out at the rate of a jar a month. On Christmas Day 1948 he put the last of them on the table: pears flavoured with cloves. I had roasted a duck, and to go with it I had a bottle of champagne. (I had paid five pounds for it to Charlie Inverarity's father, who had black market "connections".) My father was carving the duck. I put the green bottle in front of him and stood back to watch.

"What's this, Paul?" He peered hard through his glasses.

I had meant to be casual, but I said excitedly, "Champagne. The best wine in the world."

"Well," my father said. He picked up the bottle. "Is it meant to be cold like this?" He was still puritan enough to be uneasy—he was almost afraid. Champagne belonged to the world of furs and diamond tiaras, chauffeurs, courtesans, caviare. The "downtrodden poor" must also have been in his mind. "Let's save it, shall we?"

"It's your present, Dad. We're going to drink it now."

"Well." He began slowly to be pleased.

"Can I see?" Andrew said.

My father handed the bottle to him. "Champagne, Andrew. Think of that."

Andrew read the label, then turned the bottle round and read the serving instructions. "Where did you get it?"

"The black market. I've got connections." I took the bottle from him. "The cork's supposed to go pop, Dad."

Andrew stood up. He had a heavy way of making points. Angry ones came as a rule at the end of a long "slow burn". He was, I saw, slow burning now. Oh God, I thought, not today. Not after all the cooking I've done.

"Don't you think," he said, "that on this day of all days we could have some Christian feeling in the place?"

"Just let's eat our dinner," I said.

"What do you think she would have thought about this?" (He rarely called her "Mother".) "Champagne. You know how she felt about drink. You know, Dad. She was hardly dead before Paul started bringing it into the house."

"We all have to make our own decisions, Andrew," Father said.

"That means forgetting her, doesn't it? Pretending she never existed. I can hardly believe this is the house she lived in. Look at it. Filth." (A blow at my university English texts lying on the sideboard: he must have looked into *Ulysses*.) "Nothing but dirt and filth. How do you think she would have felt? And her pantry full of garlic and foreign muck. All this muck Paul's been cooking."

"Sit down, Andrew," Father said.

"And now this—this French stuff—from the black market, from criminals, on Christ's birthday. Did you know that's made by monks?"

"It's not," I said.

"It was invented by monks. And you bring it here on Christmas Day." He made a grab for the champagne but I pulled it away. He picked up the jar of pears instead. "I'm not putting this back on the table till you get rid of that."

"Sit down, Andrew," my father said. "Sit down and try to behave like an adult." From him this was a sharp rebuke.

Andrew started to cry, mostly I think with rage. "Neither of you loved her. You didn't understand what she was. I'm not staying here with you. I'm going. There are people who loved her. I'm going to live with them." He rushed to the door. "You disgust me, both of you. I'll never forgive you for what you did to her." He went out and slammed the door so hard the crockery rattled on the table. From the window my father and I watched him run down the road, with the jar of pears tucked under his arm like a football.

"Go after him, Paul," Father said.

"He'll be going to the Webbers." (Friends of Mother.)

"See if you can catch him."

"The dinner's going cold. I spent hours cooking that stuff."

A short time later Claude Webber rang and told us Andrew would spend the rest of the day with them. Father was distressed when he came from the phone. "He asked what I'd done to the boy. As if I'd beaten him."

"Come on, Dad. Let's eat something."

"Poor Andrew. I never knew he felt like that."

"It's not your fault, Dad." I had not known either. I'd seen only his disapproval; and was guilty now at the pleasure I'd taken in provoking it. I got my father back to the table. The duck was barely warm. We decided to leave the champagne for the evening meal.

"Do you really think your mother would have disapproved of this?"

"Yes," I said. I didn't want to talk about it. "If Andrew says so. He'd know."

Father belched lightly. He apologized. "It's very rich food. She thought food should be plain—close to nature. Self-consecrated, in a sense. Fuel for the body, nothing more, and the body of course is the temple of the soul, God's property. Mustn't have it reeking of garlic."

I laughed and he looked at me reprovingly. "Your mother had a great soul. I suppose Andrew's got one too. They can be painful. We'll have to try to help him, Paul."

"How?"

Claude Webber drove Andrew home in the evening. They came inside and stood in the centre of the room, rather like

87

client and lawyer. Claude Webber, a forthright man, said, "Andrew would like to come and board with us."

My father looked as if he'd been struck. For a moment he said nothing. "Is that what you want, Andrew?"

Andrew was pale. (He had grown to be bigger than me, nearly six feet tall. A softness about his flesh was accentuated by his lack of colour. His pale hair, faintly tinged with red, he kept close to his head with water. Whenever I saw him behind the teller's grille in the bank where he worked I thought of a prisoner made white and soft by bad food and lack of light and air. Yet he was physically strong, he liked being out of doors, he liked using his body. If he had been quicker he would have been formidable. But his movements seemed always to follow a pause, as though the message setting them off had trouble getting through.) He looked at my father. His eyes were red from crying.

"I don't feel this is her house any more."

It was part of Father's new doctrine that decisions must be free. He said only, "You've thought about it?"

"I don't feel this is her house any more."

"All right, Andrew."

"I'd like to lock her room."

"All right."

Claude Webber helped him pack. Everything he owned went into a suitcase and an apple-box. He locked our mother's room.

"Come back as often as you can," Father said.

"I'll be back to feed the fowls." He was not being cruel. He had known the things he must say and was saying them by rote.

"Good-bye, Father. Good-bye, Paul."

When he had gone we tried to cheer ourselves up by drinking champagne. It made us light-headed and led us to easy judgements. Andrew would come to his senses. Andrew would soon be back. With our last glass we drank solemnly to the memory of my mother.

88

I was sitting on an apple box in my stall reading *The Brothers Karamazov* when a girl wearing tennis clothes and carrying a racket walked down past the vineyard. She stopped in the middle of the swing-bridge and looked at the water. I watched through a hole in the coal-sack wall; appraising. Girls were a herd I roped prize heifers from—such was my non-satiric belief—and this one looked as if she might be prize. Good legs, certainly—long and smooth. Light brown hair that shone in the sun. Meditative. That was good. Girls should not be dumb, they should be able to appreciate my cleverness. After a while, thinking no one could see her, she lifted the side of her skirt and scratched her behind. I found the act delightful. It gave me confidence she would have a pretty face.

In a moment she turned and came on. The bridge bounced lightly to her step. Fifty more yards—her face was clear. My confidence was justified. It was natural, I suppose, that at nineteen I should prefer prettiness to character, or even beauty, in a woman's face. This one had prettiness, abundantly. She was, I remember thinking, like a grown-up Shirley Temple.

I called in a bastard accent I thought funny at the time, "You lik'a da buy da apple? Gravenstein. Fresh from da tree."

She stopped. She looked once at me, once at the apples; ignored my jokiness. "Yes," she said, "that's exactly what I feel like."

Her directness threw me out of my stride. My patter fell to Kiwi and had a stilted sound. "They're very nice apples, these. The best early season apples. Really juicy. I can recommend them." Meanwhile I was choosing the ripest one for her.

"How much?" She had taken a tiny brown purse from her cardigan pocket.

"No charge. On the house."

It was foolish: her look let me see it. She put sixpence in my hand and took the apple. "You can make up the change with plums."

"Right." I put half a dozen in a bag. "Try one."

"All right. Thank you."

I had left *The Brothers Karamazov* where she could read the title: no harm in advertizing myself. She put her racket on it. It simply wasn't there. I was chastened. I asked her name.

"Joyce Poole."

"You're new here, aren't you?"

"We came before Christmas. My father's the new Postmaster."

She told me she was eighteen. She worked as a doctor's receptionist in Avondale, but was going to look for a job in Wadesville. Wadesville was nice, it was pretty. She liked the orchards. (I smiled complacently.) She didn't like tennis much. She had joined the club so she could meet some people. Tennis made her ankles sore.

Simply by asking questions I won ascendancy. Joyce's poise was learned. She put it off the instant she felt liked. Underneath she was earnest and naive. Her eyes were deep blue, and always a little troubled—she was ready for retreat to that ice-cold poise. In this she would wait anxiously for the signal to come out. Only rarely would she use it as a weapon.

I told her I had never cared for tennis. Swimming was the sport I liked. There was a swimming hole at the back of the orchard, I said. No one knew of it but me. There was even a willow tree to dive off.

"Come for a swim tomorrow afternoon. I'll close the stall."

"Oh no, you mustn't do that."

"There's a shed here you can change in. All you need is togs and a towel." I saw, almost with fright, that she took it as an order.

We arranged a time. Then she said good-bye, blushing lightly, drew her poise about her (it gave the impression of

90

lightening her colour), took her fruit, and went off down the road. She had smooth brown legs and bony ankles I later thought aristocratic. Her behind had a demure action— maidenly. I let myself picture fading crescents on the warm orb she had scratched. (It was my first and, for weeks, only lascivious thought about Joyce Poole.) Her hair came down in a bright waterfall over her powder-blue cardigan. I never questioned the curls. She ate her apple delicately. In her other hand she carried racket and plums. She did not wave at the corner.

I went over the boys she would meet at tennis. I didn't do well in free competition but liked to work in private. I consoled myself that my move was made: tomorrow at least was sure.

The next afternoon we sat side by side at the swimming hole. Things went badly. Midnight fantasy, amazingly pure, had turned Joyce Poole into Princess to my Wadesvillean Prince. I was moved by notions of duty and prerogative. So in the afternoon I was courteous, formal, witless. I was "in love", though I had sense enough not to tell her. We swam in the murky waters of Wadesville creek. She swam badly, with childish strokes, her chin high out of the water. I churned round and round her in an agitated way. Her awkwardness marred her perfection; then became part of it.

We sat on towels and made halting conversation. To fill a silence cymbal-clashing between us I told her there were lobsters in the creek. (Good taste kept me from mentioning the eels.) She said, "Oh." To fill a second I cried, "Look," and ran like a monkey up the willow tree and jack-knifed into the deepest part of the pool. "Do something," I yelled to myself under water. She filled a third by asking what my job was. I told her I was a student. She couldn't comprehend an arts degree, even when I described the parts of it. "What do you do it *for*?" she wanted to know.

I had another swim. She declined—those lobsters. She

never swam in Wadesville creek again. We walked in the orchard. I climbed apple trees to bring her perfect apples until she reminded me with a desperate laugh that she only had two hands. Her desperation saved us. I saw she was struggling as hard as I. She was frightened, life was hostile. As plain as a written instruction she was begging me to save her. I took the apples from the pouch of arms she had made and put them at the foot of a tree. I took her hand. We walked a little further. Then I kissed her chastely on the lips. Her response was a kind of inward collapse. She was all warmth, all trust, all surrender. And I was the passionate perfect gentleman. She trusted. I was worthy. She surrendered. I took her hand. We strolled through the orchard. From time to time we exchanged soft simple kisses. At the end of an hour we were able to say we thought we were falling in love.

Joyce gave up playing tennis. On Saturdays she worked in my fruit stall. She was brisk and business-like. On the second Saturday she brought along an old pair of post office scales. From then on I sold by weight instead of number, and saw my profits climb. She put a hand-bell in the stall. On sunny afternoons we lay out the back on a blanket, kissing all the while, purse-lipped, with varying intensity. The bell rang. She pulled on a pair of gloves and ran off to make a sale; came back with a special plum which she offered to my mouth with an ungloved hand. This was the time of rewards in our affair—a time of marvellous silliness. We explored each other from the throat up and from the elbows down. (I caressed her ankles once, but saw I had gone too far.)

"I love you, Joyce."

"I love you, Paul."

I was proud of the ease with which I slew the tiny dragons of lust that sprang to life in my loins. Soon, I said, wait, not long now; striking off their heads. Zing, went my little sword, and blood reversed its motion. Soon. I gazed in Joyce's deep blue eyes and wanted nothing more for the moment.

On Saturday nights I took her to the pictures. I, who was reading *The Idiot*, agreed that *Dangerous Moonlight* was beautiful, profound. We drove to Muriwai in my father's Ford Prefect. The huge waves frightened her, the desolate track of sand vanishing into haze made her feel unhappy. I drove her home, tenderly aware of how much she needed me. The next Sunday we went to Mission Bay, where she swam happily in the six-inch waves and kept a critical eye on the new season's bathing suits. I was proud to see how people (other men) looked at her. Hands off, I said, dropping mine on her shoulders.

My father met Joyce one Saturday at the stall. He had asked me about my "new girl"; I had told him things were serious, I was in love. He dropped by casually to look her over. I'd forgotten how shy he was with women. They both blushed when I introduced them. Then Joyce fitted her murderous poise about her, and my father talked jerkily about the glorious weather. He went away soon. The only comment he made that night was that she seemed to be a "lady". Joyce, I saw, was shaken by my father's ugliness. She said he was "nice". For an hour or so she worried about my ugliness. But mine, she must have told herself then, was interesting, it made me seem strong, different, clever, hers; it woke a gentle lust in her innocent nature. So everything was soon all right again. We sold fruit. We kissed. We held hands. We went to an Abbott and Costello movie.

Three more weeks went by. The "soon" began to change shape; became "very soon"; became, one afternoon in the orchard, "now". I had shown her the den that day. She said Henry Bear was ugly, and *Hope* profound. She didn't notice the books. We closed the stall and took our rug to the bottom of the orchard. No girl had seen the den before. There was only one way of possession left to take.

We lay on the blanket and kissed in our usual way. I told her I loved her. And on the strength of that, put my hand on her breast. She let it stay. I kissed her deeply. She responded, looked at me with surprise, came back. I stroked her body outside her clothes; and did not neglect to say that I wanted to marry her. "Yes," she said in a frightened voice, frightened not at this.

After an hour of forward stepping, subtle or naive, and shifts of clothing, cunningly made, I lay on her in a gentlemanly way and made the small penetration her virgin state allowed. And there I stayed for a long while, gazing at her closed eyes. I would not hurt her, I promised; we would wait, we would only go a little way at a time, only when she felt like it. (Hero of the latest manual I'd read was Considerate Husband.) She made no reply. From time to time her body gave a delicate shiver. Then she opened her eyes and looked at me with fright. She shivered again and moaned three or four times; then lay still and quiet. I looked at her, open-mouthed. It wasn't true. She had had an orgasm. I began to climb off, but she said, "No," and held me where I was. So I did my thinking there. I was shocked. Nice girls didn't have orgasms —not so easily, not so soon. And those involuntary shivers— had they been, after all, controlled? Had I been used? But soon, looking at her pink averted face, I was able to believe that a huge compliment had been paid me. Even nice girls, even Joyce—and when I'd hardly been trying! She must be crazy about me. *Mine.*

"Do you hate me?" she asked.

"I love you."

"I'm not a bad girl."

"Of course not." I tried to think of something comforting. "You're still a virgin."

She considered this. I saw her agree. "I feel so much closer to you now."

"So do I." Nevertheless, it was time to get off. At once tender and proprietorial, I pulled down the front of her dress. *Demi-vierge*, I thought. That "demi" made her mine.

94

For the rest of the afternoon we talked and kissed and wrestled. We hopped back and forth like birds from late to early adolescence. She ran shrieking through the apple trees. I brought her down with a flying tackle—boy; and man I thought, gazed in her eyes and asked, "When will you tell your parents?" Once, lying half across her (both flushed from running), I said, "Come my Celia, let us prove, While we may, the sports of love."

"What?" she said.

"Time will not be ours for ever: He, at length, our goods will sever. It's a poem I wrote for you."

"Liar."

"I did."

"Why did you call me Celia, then?"

Her mood changed. She said the poem was beautiful and asked me to say it again. So, holding her under me, I recited without a blush,

> *"Come my Celia, let us prove,*
> *While we may, the sports of love;*
> *Time will not be ours for ever:*
> *He too soon our goods will sever."*

"It's profound." She was quiet. "Time will not be ours for ever."

"Don't get unhappy, now."

"Why is poetry always about sad things?"

At half-past five I put the blanket over our shoulders and we walked up to the house. Andrew was feeding his fowls as we went past the fowl-run. He scattered the last of the wheat and stood looking at us with a kind of dogged outrage as we went past the wire. I realized that the blanket over our shoulders had belonged to mother. I slipped out of it.

With a feeble attempt at jocularity, I said, "Andrew, this is Celia—I mean Joyce."

He came to the gate and let himself out. His movements

were so clumsy and his face so still, thickened somehow, I thought he looked imbecilic. Joyce smiled at him. She offered her hand through the opening in the blanket. "How do you do?" she said.

Andrew looked at her heavily for a moment. "My hands have got wheat on them." He turned and walked away.

That night I borrowed my father's car and took Joyce to the Fruitgrowers' Ball. Waiting in her sitting-room, I endured the scrutiny of her anxious Dad and Mum. I passed: my hair was short in those days, my ugliness was young, an out-of-doors kind. I wore the expression I called my "glow of decency". Above all, my prospects were good: so said my varsity scarf.

"Look after my girl," Mr. Poole said.

I promised.

Joyce wore a simple white three-quarter gown and a black Spanish-lace shawl. It was a great triumph for me when I saw Charlie Inverarity's black little eyes take a radar fix on her as we entered the hall. The match between us was still going on—right through our friendship it had gone on—and now I could call myself winner. There was only one Joyce Poole and she was mine. Charlie understood.

The committee had tried to decorate the hall like a barn/packing shed/saddler's shop. Country objects hung on the walls. The band sounded like a sawmill. It was playing a fox-trot when we came in. I took Joyce formally in my arms and we danced. In the years since my mother's death I had learned to dance fairly well. But Joyce was so light I hardly knew she was there. Her movements were oiled. When I told her how fantastic she was she smiled complacently and said she had a medal for ballroom dancing. We spun magnificently in front of Charlie.

After the foxtrot he came across the hall to us—in a curved line, homing in. It was a way of stating a purpose; fair warning. Confident, I introduced him to Joyce. He asked her short, gruff questions. How long had she been in Wadesville? What did she do for a living? How had she met old Paul Prior, here? Joyce was embarrassed. Then she drew her poise about her; became cool, faintly amused. I let my amusement show. But Charlie was no quitter. Doggedly he asked Joyce for the next dance.

"I've promised the first three to Paul," she smiled.

"All right, the one after that?"

"Perhaps. Come back then."

He went away—outside for a drink, I said. But she was troubled and could not relax.

"He's funny."

"How, funny?"

"Creepy."

I smiled with delight. We danced another two dances. She began to enjoy herself again. Charlie came back and claimed her. The dance was an excuse-me. I soon got her away from him.

"Thank you. What a clown."

"What did he say?"

She giggled. "I shouldn't tell you."

"Come on."

"He said he was worth two of Paul Prior any day."

"The bastard."

"Don't swear."

"The poor little dope."

"I'm not going to dance with him again. Do you mind?"

I didn't. The lights went out during the supper waltz. We kissed until we almost fainted.

The dance after supper was a three-step polonaise, "to shake down all that food", the M.C. said. Joyce and I spun like Catherine wheels. Her bright excited face slipped from my sight, I went on to my next partner; danced, spun, moved on. Then I saw Joyce running from the hall, and

Charlie standing stiff where she had left him. I shook my partner off. "What did you do to her?" I yelled.

He looked at me without expression, shrugged. I ran past him, out into the parked cars. I saw the white of Joyce's dress as she went down the line towards the Prefect. The silk of her shawl glittered in the light; the clip that fastened her hair winked like an eye.

"Joyce." I caught up with her. "What happened? What did he say?"

She got in the car and shivered. "I'm cold."

I closed the door and went round the driver's side. "Did he touch you?"

"No."

"What did he say, then? Tell me."

"Nothing."

"Why did you run?"

"I got dizzy. I thought I was going to be sick."

"Are you all right now?"

"I want to go home."

"Joyce——"

"Take me home, please."

"I'll murder that little bastard."

"It wasn't him. Take me home. Please, Paul."

On the way she leaned on her door. "I don't feel like talking," she said. I stopped in front of her house. I tried to embrace her, but she got out quickly.

"Good night, Paul. I'm sorry." Then she was gone. She was letting herself into the house before I could reach the gate.

"I'll call you tomorrow," I cried.

No reply. The porch light went out.

So I lost Joyce Poole. She wasn't home when I called the next day. On Monday her father told me on the phone that she didn't want to see me again: if I was a gentleman (he was sure I was) I wouldn't pester her. She must have known I would try an ambush. It took me three days to learn her new timetable. I stepped gangster-like from a shop doorway and said, "Don't try to get away." She gave a small shriek. Then she stared at me like a fly faced by a jumping spider. She knew she was caught, but in the fly's drugged way hoped that if she turned round and wobbled away everything might be all right, I might vanish.

I grabbed her arm. She started to buzz. "How dare you? Take your hands off me. I don't know how I could ever have thought you were a gentleman."

I could only plead. An explanation. Didn't she owe me an explanation?

"All right," she said, "all right, just let me go."

I took my hand from her arm and she started to walk quickly towards home. I tagged along at her side.

"Why didn't you tell me about your brother? Don't you think you should have told me?"

"Andrew?" I said. "What about him?" But this trailed away. Not Andrew. Of course not. John. That was what Charlie had told her in the twenty second chance the polonaise had given him. "You'd never think old Paul Prior had a loony brother." I put my hand on her arm again, urgently explained: he was dead. He had died four years ago. She need not worry, everyone had forgotten. It wasn't in the family. No, no, John was a freak, an accident. A joke of God, I joked. But I was on her side—on the side of ending. Behind our busy encounter was the tableau of myself picnicking in father's den, while up in the house John died of convulsions.

In the end I let her go; and she, I suppose, marched home to her father and mother and told them they need not be afraid of the Poole blood becoming tainted. I tried to write to her—a few facts about mongolism—but the letter always petered out. The thing was over. And although I was unhappy my aesthetic sense was pleased by the shape of this event and the way it was joined to my past.

I didn't try to see Charlie Inverarity. I could think of no

punishment for him. I guessed almost to the day when Joyce would start going out with him. (New year—she had a great sense of fitness.) By that time my father was ill. In the winter he had had an operation for an enlarged prostate. He came home, tried to go out too soon, and caught a chill. When this was over he was a tiny cavernous old man, so weak he could hardly lift a spoon. In the summer he came out into the sun and seemed to grow a little stronger. One day I found him in the den, where he had gone to fetch a book.

"It's hard to believe I spent so much of my life here." He was worried that I locked myself away. "There were so many other things I could have done."

I took his arm and we walked in the orchard. The picking gang was busy in the Gravenstein trees. One of them brought him an apple. He tried to eat it but the skin was too hard for his teeth. I went to the house for my pocket knife and cut thin slices for him.

"These trees are at their best, Paul . . . I don't think you'll end up an orchardist."

"No."

"Or Andrew."

"No."

I told him I thought I would be a teacher. He tried to develop an analogy between growing fruit and teaching children; but suddenly grew impatient with it. "I've always been light-minded. That's my trouble." He was warning me.

We sat down and enjoyed the sun. At four o'clock when we went back to the house he complained of feeling cold. By ten o'clock he was delirious. I called the doctor, who was angry with me for keeping him in the orchard so long. I have no guilt about it. He enjoyed that afternoon.

My father lingered for a week and died without any pain. On the last day he had moments of dim consciousness. In one of these he offered me a piece of his experience. "Paul," he said, "women are so damned biological."

## 1949–1967

I left Wadesville when I was twenty-one. As a tool for unlocking the world my arts degree turned out to be blunt. It opened chalky classrooms. Other equipment I carried proved more useful: my knowledge of how to make a den and hibernate; kitchen skill; an armour of generalizations about women. I built a *persona* that gave an impression of toughness. "What you've got to do," I said, "is get rid of your sense of justice"—this usually to people I was hurting, but also to Paul Prior when hurt (a rare event, at last). I cultivated detachment. The years went easily, with some pleasure, a little pain. I found myself quite often in a state of honest self-approval. "You're getting by," I said, "you're minding your own business. People should be more reasonable."

I taught in a country town for two years, in Wellington for two; in Sydney; in Vancouver. I taught English in Italy. I lived four years in a flat in Ladbroke Grove and came to believe myself a Londoner. My only news of Wadesville came from Andrew. He wrote each year on our mother's birthday ("she'd be upset if she thought we were strangers to each other") and at Christmas. I replied on postcards showing cathedrals, bullfights, vineyards, Gauguin nudes. He told me he was still living with the Webbers—he called them Uncle and Auntie—and working in the bank. Wadesville was booming. There were shops going up all along the road between the bridges. The orchard had been zoned as industrial land. Claude Webber thought we should sell when the lease ran out. The Apple and Pear Marketing Board had made an offer for ten acres, a battery factory and a timber yard wanted the rest. The sums offered were huge. Sell, I wrote back. The idea of holidays in luxury hotels intoxicated me. Later I thought of paintings and rare books and wine in cobwebby bottles. But at last what moved me was the thought of bulldozers knocking down the original den and tearing out the fruit trees I had lain on blankets under with Joyce Poole. Sell, I told Andrew. I gave him power of attorney.

In the letter in which he told me the orchard was sold Andrew announced his engagement to the Webber's niece, Penelope. He sent me a snapshot of them taken in the back yard. She was a pretty girl, though she had a butter-fed look. She reminded me of Miss Weaver, with whom I had been in love for a day. Their styles too seemed roughly the same: twin-set, artificial pearls, permed hair. Her home life, Andrew told me, wasn't all it should be. Her mother (the Webber) was a Theosophist, her father had taken refuge in science fiction. Some of this had rubbed off on Penelope. But since she had come to live with the Webbers, said Andrew, she had started to think more correctly. The political phrase surprised me. Did it mean Andrew's religion was now on the surface of his mind? I hoped so. I sent my congratulations on a card showing Botticelli's *Birth of Venus*.

A year after his marriage Andrew came up with "a gilt-edged proposition". He had bought a small furniture factory on the North Shore. The market was wide open; he could sign a dozen contracts tomorrow. The problem was expansion. More capital was needed. Although investors were clamouring, he had made up his mind to give me first chance. It would be, on his honour, like buying shares in a gold mine. And *Priors*, he felt, should be a family concern. Our mother would have wanted it. Father too, he supposed.

The after-thought nearly made me stay out. But I cooled

down after a while. I was back from a holiday in the South of France and knew I wasn't going to make the grade as an international playboy. Luxury hotels strained my conscience: a humiliating discovery. And of course, mine was only a small amount of money. I re-did my sums and decided I would have to teach for at least half of each year. So I became part owner of a furniture factory. I came to Great Money Lake with my brand new enamel mug and conscience allowed me to stay. Others there were guarding private pipelines.

I took a job at a Grammar School and began to feel that I was a fairly good teacher. Women came into my life; complained of my hollow centre; left after a variety of scenes. I was happy most of the time. I changed flats; built a new den; had holidays in Greece and Yugoslavia. Letters arrived from Andrew. He and Penelope were "ideally suited". They were parents of a boy called Jonathan. Andrew had bought a house in Takapuna and seldom went out west any more. The changes in Wadesville grieved him. Once, driving through, he noticed that my "old boyhood friend" Inverarity had opened a big new drapers shop. The news failed to move me. Charlie was like someone I had met at a party—a bad party. And Wadesville was a foreign town.

Yet it was Wadesville that brought me back to New Zealand. In August 1962 I was on holiday in Spain. In Alicante I walked in the back-streets, a few yards from my fellow tourists. The poverty there filled me with shame. Back on the boulevard, hot and tired, I sat on a shaded seat to cool off. A man came up and charged me two pesetas. I was glad of the chance to be angry. But anger, I found, needed its feet on some native ground. The frontiersman stepped out. Pay to sit in the shade! Not likely. I'd leave their bloody clip-joint country. Head for the bush. Head for home. I had a vision of Wadesville: cool, egalitarian, green. That was where I belonged—not in this Fascist tourist-trap.

I stayed another month, though not in Alicante. All the time Wadesville kept me company. I thought of it not obsessively, not with longing; automatically. A circuit had been opened, my mind sent memories through—images more often than events. Slightly mystified, I gazed at them. What was this in aid of? I lay on a beach near Malaga and remembered Cascade Park. I watched fish struggling up an almost dry weir in Murcia and thought of tommy cods and silver bellies, silver hook and pink piece of worm vanishing into still green water. I drove through olive groves and thought of Prior's orchard. In the Alhambra I remembered the Wadesville Town Hall! But mostly it was the creek—Charlie and me in our tin canoes—pools opening out, each one like a room. I travelled from the launching place to the sea. Over an arm of mangrove swamp I saw the cliffs of the North Shore; pink castles, burning windows.

What was this about? The places I was remembering didn't exist any more. I had no home. Or if I had, it was London; the Thames was my creek. Be reasonable, I told myself, calm down. But now I could almost taste my childhood.

As I drove north through the Basque country it was plain I was heading for Wadesville.

Several months later I strolled on Takapuna beach with my brother and his wife. Ahead, Jonathan was throwing pipi shells into the wind. Jonathan had surprised me. He was a big freckled happy child who lolloped about like a puppy. After dinner he had ambushed me in the hall and taken me to his bedroom. Two postcards I'd sent from Spain were pinned to the wall.

"Have you really seen a bullfight?" he asked.

"Where did you get these?"

"Dad threw them in the waste-paper basket. He said it was your sense of humour. Is this a real castle?"

"Oh yes."

"With torture chambers and dungeons?"

"Yes. It's ruined now, though."

"Was there blood on the walls?"

"If there was any it's gone now," I said. "Aren't you scared he'll find them?"

Jonathan laughed. "He never comes in here. We saw a Maori fort last year. It was just a lot of ditches. Did this one have bullet holes?"

"No. I'll send you some cards if you like, when I go back."

"You're not going back. You've just got here."

I saw that Jonathan was going to make a hero of me. As we left the bedroom he said, "Dad says you're a tough guy."

"Not really. I'm a bit of a sissy."

He laughed as if this were a huge joke. "You're not like a teacher."

On the beach Andrew said again, "You should have told us, Paul. Just walking in when we thought you were round the other side of the world. It's too much."

"Andrew," Penelope said, "do stop harping on it. He's told us he's sorry."

"Yes, but after fifteen years. . . ." Andrew was affronted. My behaviour criticized him. He was also a little awed that twelve thousand miles and fifteen years could be so casually treated. It surprised me to find his voice slipping back to the aggrieved tone of his adolescence. The change in him was greater than I had expected. He was a hard, quick, determined man—unflappable, to use his wife's term. Yet I had the uneasy sense that my coming had shifted a balance in him. He reminded me, as he talked, of our mother in disapproving vein. There was also something of Father: a wobble in purpose, an over-quickness of mind. I had given him a glimpse of—freedom?—anarchy? Self-indulgence! Only in moments of pause did he know what he thought.

As we reached the end of the beach Penelope asked me my plans. Penelope disapproved of me too. She was in love with order. But after her "flap" when I knocked at the door she had got me safely into a cage marked "Eccentric relatives—Andrew's side". Now, though she disapproved, she was pleased to have me. There was nothing malicious in this—I was not to be a weapon against Andrew—it simply satisfied her hunger for order to have a brother of his making weight opposite her space-wandering Dad and Theosophist Mum.

We turned and walked back towards the house. I told them I'd probably behave like a tourist for a while. I had never been to the South Island. Penelope nodded approvingly: the South Island should be collected.

"Are you going to have a look at Wadesville?" Andrew said. There was still a note of complaint in his voice: Wadesville too obeyed no rules. "The place seems to have gone crazy. I can't find my way around it any more."

I said I would probably take a drive out that way for old time's sake. Penelope nodded again. "Roots," she said in a satisfied voice. Andrew glanced at her sharply, then looked at me. "The orchard's gone. Completely."

"But the money's in the bank," I said.

"Yes." He was angry. The equation worked in some other way for him. "Your friend Inverarity's done well. He's got a big shop in a block he owns. He must be making a fortune in rent."

"Charlie was born a winner," I said.

"He married that girl you used to take out. The one who looked like an Indian."

"Indian? You mean Joyce Poole?"

He shrugged; he didn't know her name. It was several minutes before I understood: American Indian. I almost shouted with laughter. That blanket of our mother's, that was what he remembered, not Joyce Poole. I told him Charlie wasn't my friend any longer, he'd pinched my girl. I was on the edge of describing the trick, but remembered Andrew's feeling for John in time. Besides—did Penelope know about our brother? Asking this, I felt I'd come a long way back to concerns I'd thought myself rid of as surely as childhood warts and adolescent pimples. The tainted Prior blood. The facts about Down's syndrome should be taught in schools, I thought, along with the facts about sex. All the same, Penelope probably had been told. Andrew had never shared my shame; he had out-stripped me there. A turn-up for the books—I was supposed to bear enlightenment's torch. Consider him now though, frowning, looking lemonish, calling his wife's attention to the sunset, because a girl in a skimpy bathing suit walked across their path. "The drawback of this beach is the people," Andrew said. "The prices we pay for our properties, you'd think we could have some privacy. It's our rates that maintain the place—and all the riff-raff of Auckland come and mess it up." He gestured at the girl, who gave a squeal as she dipped her bum in the water. Then he stood still and pointed to his house, squatting among its peers. "Do you know what I paid for that place? Eleven thousand pounds. You don't pay that sort of money to have your view cluttered up with . . ." (a life-saving practice, strollers kissing). "I had an offer of seventeen thousand last week. I'm thinking seriously about taking it."

"There should be a part of the beach for the property holders," Penelope said. "Surely that would be fair. The council could put up a wall."

"Or lay a mine-field," I said.

Andrew frowned and said coldly, "It's all very well for you, Paul. You don't have to live here. If my wife wasn't with us I'd tell you some of the things that go on."

I apologized. We went back to the house and had coffee. Jonathan said he hoped I'd be coming to see them again. He shook hands and went to bed. Penelope took out her knitting. I asked her if she unravelled it at night. She gave a puzzled smile, and changed it to a social one when I explained. "I've never seen the point of those old-fashioned stories."

Andrew brought out his books. He began to explain my investment. I protested: I had no head for these things, I trusted him completely. Besides, my lawyer looked after my interests.

"You've put your money in, Paul," he said. "Now it's your duty to understand."

It was midnight before he let me go.

Wadesville shone like a glossy magazine. Driving slowly from bridge to bridge through a gully walled with plate-glass and coloured tile I told myself that none of it fooled me. I'd seen too much, I'd seen the world. This was not a suburb, this was still a town. The Golden Mile was the Great North Road tarted up; two storeys in place of one, glass and tile in place of weather-board. I had the sense of rusty iron, countryside, behind the facade: orchards, vineyards, blackberry patch and cowyard. Nevertheless, I was prepared to be affectionate, in a patronizing way. I looked for people I had known. The streets were full of sunburned men in shorts and women pushing prams. I felt a little put out: someone should have welcomed me. I was important—I carried knowledge of this town's infancy.

I drove into the factory belt to find Prior's orchard. I knew what to expect, but the completeness of the blotting-out struck me like a blow. I felt sick. Not a tree, not a blade of grass—no den, no house, not even a fragment of rotten timber. Huge fibrolite cool-stores set on asphalt yards. A glass office with two secretaries, pretty and plain. Trucks. Gloomy vistas of cased fruit. It cheered me a little to see that the old swing-bridge was still in use. But in spite of my childhood crossings of it, and my first sight of Joyce Poole, the bridge had never lived in my imagination. The creek did that, the orchard and the den. I went on to the bridge and looked at the creek: a ditch of grey scummy water with islands of detergent froth moving on its surface. Nothing could be alive in it. A smell of decay came up, more chemical than organic. I cleared my throat and spat hurriedly.

So much, I thought, for coming home.

I went to my car and drove back to the shopping area. In a last effort to whip up my nostalgia I looked for the name Inverarity; and wondered then how I had missed it earlier. The shop stood on the corner section where the boarding-house had been. Inverarity Buildings: the name was raised in bright red concrete letters above the veranda. I wondered how Charlie had prospered to this degree. It struck me that his book-making father must have done very well. At this memory of a man I had hardly known and never liked—a sour, spiky little man accepting betting slips in a shop that smelled of cloth and camphor—my stomach fluttered at last. Nostalgia. The genuine article. I was pleased with myself. I thought it might be entertaining to see what Charlie looked like behind a counter.

Inside the shop it was cool and bright. Charlie (or perhaps Joyce) had gone in for display. One side was given to women's wear, the other to men's and boys'. Shelves of rolled dress and curtain materials made a multi-coloured bank across the end wall. I counted a staff of eight. Charlie came at me out of a bay I had missed, using the sidling, slightly crooked approach that seemed to state a purpose.

"Hello, Paul. What brings you back this way?"

We shook hands. I was conscious of making my grip hard, something I hadn't done since a boy. "Just looking at the old town. It's changed."

We conversed like this for several minutes. Charlie ran through Wadesville's growth, I my travels. I saw that his vice was decision. Everything he said was flat; there was about it something clipped and brutal. This marked no change, I thought, this was simply the boy become man. He had found a stance and not let it change. Like Andrew's, his face had less bulk, but where Andrew's had grown thinner

Charlie's seemed to have shrunk. His hair still bristled like a black shoe-brush. His eyes were cold and bright—more vivid because of the brownness of his face. I wondered if he used a sun-lamp.

There was still a contest between us; the one that had started on that summer day in the playground and run submerged through our friendship. Yes Charlie, I wanted to say, you won the farting competition all right but don't forget I won the long-distance pissing. He looked at me with a smile that barely hid contempt.

"How's Joyce?" I asked.

"Fit and well." A straight counter-blow—no waste.

"Any children?"

"Two."

"Does she still like apples?" I saw the absurdness of what I was doing. I decided to stop—declare the contest off. Hadn't I pushed involvement out of my life? "Anyway," I said, "I'm glad you're doing so well." I waved my hand at the busy staff. It was then I saw the woman watching us from the small glassed-in office in a back corner of the shop. It was like seeing a face under water. Joyce Poole. Joyce Inverarity. She was smiling slightly. Her cheeks were red with embarrassment.

"Hallo," I said.

She came out of the office. "I wasn't sure you'd remember me."

"Of course I do." I did not remember her like this. I felt a surge of joy as I saw how she had thickened—face, body, legs. The ankles that had been "aristocratic" were swollen and had no shape. They looked painful. I remembered how they had troubled her at tennis.

"You look well, Joyce."

She gave a dry smile. "So do you." I saw that one of her front teeth had turned grey. Thirty-five, I thought, she looks forty-five.

"What brings you back to Wadesville?"

"Oh," I said, "I'm just having a look at the old town. Thought I'd like to see where the orchard was." I had not meant to remind her of our afternoons there. The pink on her face deepened. Where, I thought, was her poise? She smiled, and one of her hands came up to cover the dead tooth—a movement I saw she wasn't conscious of. I found the flaws in her self-possession moving and wanted to say something to set her at ease.

"Is your father still Postmaster?"

She shook her head. "He died last year."

"I'm sorry."

Charlie said, "How's Andrew?"

"He's well. He's on the Shore."

"Married? By the way, you're not, are you?"

"I'm the one that got away." I managed a fair degree of lightness. "Andrew's got a son. A bright little chap."

"Oh yes?"

"Top of his class at school." I smiled at Joyce. "Charlie tells me you've got two children."

"Yes."

"Boys? Girls?"

"One of each."

"How old are they?"

"Ralph's thirteen." She looked around with a trace of desperation. "This one's eleven." A child was walking towards us with a sullen expression on her face. She stopped at Joyce's side. "When are you coming, Mum?" she complained.

"In a minute, dear. You wait outside."

"I'm tired of waiting."

What an unattractive child, I thought. Her face seemed to combine the worst features of her parents': an exaggeration of Joyce's prominent mouth, the antagonistic glitter of Charlie's eyes. "I always have to hang around," she said.

"Go and get me some cigarettes," Charlie said. He found something improper in the mixture of persons. The girl looked more sullen, but held out her hand, and Charlie put money in it. She slumped away to the door.

"Celia," Charlie called.

"What?"

"Get a box of matches too."

Defeat I would have shrugged off; left to take up my life again round the other side of the world. Victory was too much for me. Joyce was looking at me with an expression of fright. "What a nice old-fashioned name," I said. I smiled at her. Then, without looking at Charlie—I might have laughed aloud—I made an excuse and went out of the shop.

In the street the girl was dawdling towards a tobacconist shop. Her hair was done in pigtails so tight I thought they must be painful. They were knotted with red ribbons at the ends. *Come my Celia, let us prove, While we may the sports of love*. . . . She suddenly swung her leg like a fullback and booted an ice-cream carton on to the road. The wind from a passing bus rolled it back to the gutter. This made her grin with delight, and she skipped the rest of the way to the tobacconist shop. I went to my rented car and drove to Auckland.

My cup runneth over, I thought. I saw a future in which I would pass daily under Charlie's nose knowing what I knew: the child was mine as surely as if she had been conceived that afternoon in the orchard.

Joyce had handed me Charlie on a platter.

Six months later I had my house on its acre of ground. My den was full of books freighted from London. Henry Bear was on the mantelpiece and *Hope*, joky *Hope*, on the wall. What I did not have was Charlie. I did not even think of him. The only Inverarity I saw was Ralph, whom I taught at Wadesville College. He was a tough rowdy boy, with a stupidity deeper but less noticeable than his cleverness. He nicknamed me Pansy because I refused to coach a football team.

I found that Wadesville, old Wadesville, lived a kind of ghetto life inside the new. I surprised it in corners, in old streets, old buildings, old faces. I bought fruit at roadside stalls and wine from a Dalmatian up the valley. The Presbyterian church stood on the hill, the old primary school on its asphalt yard in a litter of new prefabricated classrooms. I bought my clothes from one of Charlie's competitors, but we nodded when we met in the street. Once we chatted for five minutes in a queue at the bank. He took my settling in Wadesville as a compliment—the town seemed to live for him the way the orchard and creek had for me. I felt no hostility towards him: our last bout, I thought, had jerked me out of an adolescence chronically prolonged. With no malice, I asked after Joyce's health. She wrote to me, excusing Ralph from homework. *Dear Paul . . . Joyce Inverarity*. From time to time I saw her in the street, sometimes with her pigtailed daughter. My feeling about her preserving that afternoon in the orchard was a mixture of conceit and pity. Life must be dry with Charlie.

When I had been two years at Wadesville College Celia Inverarity appeared in my third form English class. She drifted through the year in eighteenth place out of thirty-five. On her report I wrote the lazy remark: *Must try harder*. It embarrassed me that I had once, if only for a moment, thought of myself as begetter of this child.

"What's the new Inverarity like?" someone asked in the staffroom.

"Stodgy," I replied.

She seemed to be in a kind of puberal sleep from which she could wake only to days of complaint and stubbornness. She passed out of my class, and for the next year I was aware of her only when my notice was jogged.

"She's got a nasty tongue, that girl."

"Intelligence is no excuse."

Intelligence? I couldn't really believe it. But at the end of the year she won prizes for English and French. Joyce and Charlie came to the prize-giving. Watching Joyce's satisfied smile and the black glitter of Charlie's eyes, I remembered for the first time in two years that I had means to hurt them.

We met outside the hall after the ceremony. They thanked me for helping Ralph, who had been in my lower sixth history class.

"He's had a good year," I said. "Any idea what you're going to be yet Ralph?"

"A lawyer," he said flatly, and looked away over my head.

"Celia's done well." It was the first time I had spoken her name to Joyce. She was too happy to let herself be embarrassed.

"We were so worried about her last year. We didn't know whether she was clever or not."

"She's clever, all right," Charlie said. He put his arm round Celia's waist. I saw the girl glance at her parents with pity. She moved in a kind of pirouette out of her father's arm and walked across the road to a group of friends.

Joyce smiled. "Especially your comments on the report. Celia was rather scathing about that."

"I'll bet she was."

Charlie was eyeing the fur on my bachelor's hood. "She seems to think she'll be having you for English next year."

"That's right."

"Previous." He laughed.

"What?"

"Previous Prior. That's her nickname for you." He laughed again. "I thought you'd like to know. Kids are pretty sharp these days."

The malice in his voice shocked me. There was threat too, of a vague sort. Joyce was looking angry. "We'd better go now, Charlie." I heard her voice scolding him as they walked away.

I told myself I wasn't going to be drawn into another contest. That sort of thing was behind me. I seemed on the point of finding in myself a desire to be liked. Even by Charlie. Even by his clever daughter. Previous, I thought. The little bitch. I drove home and listened to some music—a wind quartet by Danzi—but it put me on edge: all that restraint, all that formal neatness. I'd thought I had these qualities in my life, and here I was wanting to be liked by a clown like Charlie. Really, I thought, if open war's the only other course you'd better take it. But I had a second whisky and got myself in order. Detachment, self-sufficiency. Den-living. I put another record on the player and let myself be soothed. The Inveraritys were midges on some scummy private pond. I was here. The walls closed warmly in. I stroked my sideburns, sipped my whisky; listened.

In the next year I kept myself remote from Celia. It did not matter that she was the best pupil in my fifth form English class, I treated her simply as one of thirty-five and excused myself on the grounds of egalitarianism. I played the teacher even when she came to me to talk about books she was reading, even when I loaned her books, which I began to do in the middle of the year. Her sleep was over. A hunger for knowledge had woken in her. Scarcely a lesson went by but her voice interrupted with some cunning question. There was in her such an excitement, such a quick recognition of falseness, that I found myself building my answers with extraordinary care. But still I held her at arms length. On occasions I found her looking at me with amusement. In the hall one day a trick of acoustics brought me her voice across half the assembled school. "Poor old Previous, he always looks as if he's got constipation." It was after this that she began to be rebellious. She argued with me about my classroom rules—few enough—and refused at last to obey the ones she believed unreasonable. Books in the course that failed to interest her she left unread. One of her reviews said simply: "As I found this 'classic' too boring to read I am not able to write about it." This would have delighted me if the blow had been aimed at Charlotte Brontë alone. I asked other teachers if she was giving trouble. She was not. The truth is Celia was hurt. We liked the same things. We liked each other. Why then did I treat her as a child? Why did I keep on pretending to be teacher? She did not have her mother's ability to turn herself into a stony little fortress. She had to bristle; she had to fight. By the end of the second term I was feeling bruised.

Shortly after the holiday started Charlie paid me a visit. I tried to keep him on the veranda but he smiled with a diffidence strange in him and asked if we could go inside. I showed him into the den, turned on the ceiling light and turned off my reading lamp—converting the place to a sitting-room. Charlie blinked. His eyes went quickly over the books.

"I see you still read."

I invited him to sit down and offered him a drink.

"Thanks. Whisky if you run to it." He was more himself now, his diffidence tipping over into aggression. As I poured drinks his eyes kept up their probing.

"Hey, I remember that. Your old man had it." He nodded at Henry Bear. I handed him a glass of whisky. He got up and walked across to the mantelpiece. The carving seemed to fascinate him just as it had twenty-five years before. He took it down in one hand. "Clean through the middle of the chest. Where'd he get it?"

"In a second-hand shop—it reminded him of himself." I regretted saying this, but here in my own territory I needed to establish ascendancy over Charlie. I went on in a flippant tone, "He was a kind of bear too. The spear's his wife and kids. There he was minding his own business and suddenly he's got this spear rammed through his guts."

Charlie looked at me suspiciously, not quite sure of the

challenge. He put the carving back in its place. "That's the trouble with you arty blokes, you've always got to see something that isn't there." He crossed the room and sat down. "It's a bloody bear with a spear in it."

I grinned at him. "If you say so." I said nothing more, but watched him as he set his eyes darting about the room again. The vase of flowers on the mantelpiece made him pause. I saw him wondering if it meant a woman. But finally he said, "Jesus, Paul, do you really live like this?"

"How?"

"In a room full of books?"

"They're good company. You'd be surprised."

"Sure—but what about a wife? This is no way to spend your life." He waved at the shelves.

"Oh," I said, "I have women. No shortage. But they don't fit up there. I keep them in the bedroom."

He grinned—a masculine reflex. "That's okay. What about kids though? Books'll never make up for that."

I took a swallow of whisky and kept myself under control. "They last longer."

He grunted with a contempt completely genuine, and decided I wasn't worth arguing with. His eyes took on a distant look. "Anyway, that's not what I came to talk about. I want you to stop lending books to Celia. She's getting all sorts of crappy ideas in her head."

"Like what?"

"Like staying at school, and going to university. She'll get School Certificate. That's enough for a girl."

"You want her to sit in that office of yours and add up your profits?"

"It's my business what I want her to do. What I'm telling you is, stop putting phony ideas in her head. This sort of muck"—he waved his hand at the room—"never got anyone anywhere."

"Ralph's different, of course. He can be a lawyer."

"Ralph's a boy."

"I was right, wasn't I? You really want her in the shop. You think you can keep her marking time there until some neat little prick with the right sort of job and the right sort of habits comes along and asks if he can marry her."

"Listen——"

"You listen, Charlie. You haven't got a chance. That girl's going to be someone, whether you want it or not. She's worth a dozen Ralphs. Ralph's off the assembly line. You give me some scissors and paste and I'll make you a platoon of him in ten minutes. But there's only one of Celia. Go down to the school and ask any teacher. She could no more work in your shop than she could in a brothel."

He was sitting on the edge of the sofa, leaning forward as if looking for an opening. We seemed to be circling each other again, as we had in the playground thirty years before. But I had already landed blows. Then I would have felt satisfaction, not regret. I leaned back and crossed my legs. "That's it, Charlie. You can't win this one. She'll be too tough for you."

"I'm her father." He was trembling. "I say what she does."

I shook my head. "You can't put a girl like Celia in a cage."

He jumped to his feet. "You shut up about her. Don't you use her name." The violence in him frightened me. Charlie wasn't properly tamed any more than his daughter. I sat forward in my chair.

"Let me put it this way, Charlie——"

"I'm talking now. She's leaving school. I'm not letting bastards like you mess my family up any more. You think I'm going to have her end up as bloody screwloose as you—stuck in some pansy outfit like this?" Again the wave at the room. "I know what you were doing to Joyce—filling her head with shit. Poetry! Well, I'm telling you mate, you're not going to do the same thing with my daughter." He emphasized the final words with a finger that prodded inches from my face.

"Go home, Charlie," I said.

He stepped back. He flung a challenging look round the room. "I'll give you warning, Prior, if you try to interfere with my family again I'll come up here and take a bloody axe to you. Don't think I don't mean it."

"I believe you. Now go home." I was sickened by the scene—my part in it as much as his. It seemed to have no connection with Celia, whom I remembered now in her desk with a hand raised to the level of her throat as she prepared a question. Charlie looked for a place to put his glass. He pushed it roughly on to the record player. Whisky slopped over the side.

We're a couple of bloody fools, Charlie, I thought. Old men. Don't let's spoil her chance.

He went out without looking at me again. I heard his car take off like a Grand Prix racer. I'll have to get out of this town, I thought, otherwise something's going to happen.

I got a cloth and wiped up Charlie's whisky, then poured myself some more. I sat in my chair thinking, I'll have to get out of this town.

The next day I drove south. I stayed two nights in Rotorua and three in Wairakei. I admired geysers and boiling mud and soaked myself in mineral pools. By the time I came back to Wadesville Charlie was a midge again.

But my five-day cure went for nothing. On the Sunday before school started Joyce Inverarity phoned. Her voice gave me a tiny sexual shock—it had a breathless sound, it echoed along a shaft sunk into my past.

"Paul," she said, "I hope you'll forgive me ringing. I thought you might tell me what Charlie said when he came to see you."

I told her, leaving out what he'd said about her. She

thought for a moment. I heard a clicking sound and wondered if tapping that dead tooth had become another habit of hers.

"Thank you, Paul." She was hesitating. "I'm sorry we troubled you. I'll try to see he doesn't come again."

"What's happening, Joyce? Is Celia coming back?"

"Oh yes. For School Certificate. Charlie's got it fixed in his head even girls should have that."

"What about next year?"

"I don't know yet. I want her to." She paused. "It's been a dreadful week here. They've been at each other like cat and dog. He won't let her go out. She's been locked in the house all week-end."

"Look," I said, "go and see Price——"

"He hit her, Paul. She's got a cut on the inside of her mouth. I don't know what it is he wants from her—he's trying to turn her into some sort of ideal woman—some sort of Virgin Mary. He thinks more went on between you and me than actually did. He's always accusing me. And Celia's got to make up for it somehow."

"Does he know how she got her name?"

"I knew you remembered that. I'd never tell him. He'd go mad."

If I'd still been in competition with Charlie these revelations would have set me drumming on my chest. But I simply felt alarmed. "Look Joyce, go and see Price. Tell him Charlie wants the girl to leave. Price will get on to him. He's a solid citizen. Just the sort to impress Charlie."

"Paul——"

I knew I was failing her. It made me angry with both of us. "I can't help. Anything I say, Charlie'll do the opposite. You know that. Price is the only one who can help. He's not going to let a pupil who might win a scholarship get away from him. Make him tell Charlie she'll win some money— and get her name in the paper."

Joyce said nothing for a moment. "All right, Paul. I'm sorry we've given you so much trouble." Her voice was withdrawn and tired. She was apologizing for more than just the last week.

"That's all right. It's part of my job as a teacher."

Celia came back to school with a swollen mouth. Price sent for her from my class. Later he asked for special reports on her work. Price, with his bland whisky face, is a combination public relations man and hanging judge. But Charlie wasn't easy. He put Price in a temper and we (teachers and pupils) suffered a discipline drive for the rest of the week.

I let myself move a little closer to Celia. I relaxed with her; but still I was cautious, remembering Charlie, and my new ease was more of feeling than of behaviour. Her response seemed modelled on this. She worked hard at her schoolwork. There was a kind of fatigue in her emotions. She was careful to do nothing that might call them into action again. In the meantime her life was Maths, Science, English, History, French.

Mine, out of school, was given to bringing a painless end to an affair I'd been having with a woman called Marlene Wainwright. Painless for her, I mean. My emotions were not involved. Marlene was a speech therapist. (A part of our trouble was that I could never take this title seriously.) She wrote poetry that I thought rather good of its kind: earthmotherish. It was an increasing density in the poems, a kind of urgent obliqueness, that made me suspect she was trying to get pregnant. I saw there was no painless end for her. Marlene was a gin-drinker. One Saturday I made her drunk; firmly, gently—it was like preparing a patient for operation. I sat her in my armchair in the den. I told her exactly where I stood: marriage was out for me, children were out. Hadn't I made this plain right from the start? Yes, she admitted, starting to cry. Well then, I said, if we carried on it would have to be under my rules. Rule one: Take the pill. In a kind of hysteria then she told me time was getting short for her, she was thirty-seven. If she didn't have a child soon she would never have one. "Help me," she said, "give me a child. I'll go away. You'll never see me again." I said no, and she called me a bloody murderer. I remembered my mother with John, remembered Joyce, and my father's words on his death-bed. Like him I might know, but would never understand. I had nothing to offer Marlene but another glass of gin.

She ran weeping to the bedroom and threw herself face downwards on the bed. After trying to comfort her for a while I went out and closed the door. I sat in my den and tried to think how else I might have behaved. A retroactive repair job, that was what I needed—some circuit-tinkering in the time of Mother, and of Joyce. I withdrew from examining this in laziness more than fear. I began to approve my handling of the present: I kept my rules, and let other people know what they were. How could I be more fair? I had got rid of my sense of justice. Why couldn't they?

I went out to the veranda and sat in the sun. While the woman cried in the bedroom I enjoyed feelings of well-being and virtue. Her sound coming thinly through the wall was counterpoint to the discipline of my way.

As I sat there Andrew drove up and parked at the gate. He walked up the path, bringing Jonathan with him.

"Whose is that?" he asked, pointing at Marlene's Volkswagen.

"A friend of mine's."

Jonathan grinned at me. He sat on the edge of the veranda. "I can hear someone crying," he said.

"Yes. It's her. She sat on a bee."

"Honest?"

I nodded. "I had to put blue-bag on it." Andrew's presence brought out a weak facetiousness in me. Often it drew material from our childhood. Our mother had used blue-bag on our bee-stings. I guessed from Jonathan's puzzled look that the stuff probably wasn't made any longer.

Andrew said, "Can we go inside?" He wanted to get his son away from Marlene's noises. It surprised me that he didn't simply take him back to the car and drive away.

I showed them into the den and got rid of the gin bottle and glasses. Andrew watched me bitterly. He too seemed to be suffering from a sense of injustice. He must have been looking forward to this visit. It was the first he had paid me with his son.

"Come away from those," he ordered as the boy began to drift towards my books.

I went to the kitchen to make a cup of tea. Marlene had stopped crying. I heard her open the bedroom door and run to the bathroom. Voices came from the den.

"Put it down."

"Sorry."

"How often have I told you not to touch things in other people's houses?"

"Sorry."

I began to feel surrounded and was glad of the gin I'd drunk. I took the tea into the den.

"Sugar and milk, Jonathan?" He was thirteen: it was time his father started to see him as more than an infant.

"Thanks," he said, looking surprised. He was at the mantelpiece, admiring Henry Bear.

"You can take it down if you like."

He threw a grin at his father and lifted the carving over to the table. I gave him his tea and took a cup to Andrew. "Well, brother," I said, "it's nice to see you."

He sipped his tea and winced as it burnt his lips. "Penny sends her regards." He waited for me to entrust him with mine for her. I couldn't go through with the ritual. Instead I turned to Jonathan. He was nose to nose with the bear, engaged in some private dialogue.

"That belonged to your grandfather. You never met him."

"No."

"He found it in a second-hand shop. That's where he got a lot of these books."

"Put it back now," Andrew said.

Jonathan obeyed. "I wish he'd left it to us."

"I'll leave it to you. I'll put a special clause in my will."

"Honest?"

We drank our tea. At that moment Marlene pulled the chain in the lavatory. The cistern sounds like a traction engine. I'd kept it as an antique. Andrew went red. Like Swift, he's never got used to the fact that women shit. For a moment he forgot the boy was there.

"How long are you going to go on like this, Paul?"

"Women, you mean?" I shrugged. "It's a way of keeping pure in thought." Unconsciously I had used one of Mother's phrases. I picked it up almost as quickly as he. But Jonathan chose that moment to rattle his saucer. Andrew changed course.

"This. A room full of books. You're wasting your time."

The echo of Charlie astonished me. I waited for him to go on, but under Jonathan's eye he could not settle. Irritably he said, "When are you going to cut that hair off your face?"

I touched my sideburns. "Don't you like them?"

"They make you look absurd."

"I'm sorry. They give me something to play with in bed." At once I was sorry I'd said this. Jonathan turned quickly away from his father. There was a faint grin on the hidden side of his face. Andrew put down his cup. He began to stand up. "You really go too far, Paul."

But Marlene too chose this moment to leave. She was suddenly in the doorway, with her overnight bag in her hand.

"I'm leaving, Paul." Marlene was a heavy user of make-up —especially lipstick and eye make-up. The bedroom sometimes seemed ankle-deep in tissues smeared with all the

124

colours of the rainbow. Now her face was washed clean. Her lips and eyes were swollen and pale freckles showed on her cheeks. She was more attractive to me than she had been for months. I felt a deep regret at losing her.

"All right," I said. "I'm sorry."

"I made the bed." Tears burst from her eyes.

"Thank you."

"You'll never see me again." She turned and ran out of the house. The Volkswagen roared like a truck and the sound of it died away.

Andrew's face was pinched and yellow. The boy's though seemed to glow. He was looking at me with admiration. We spent the next hour driving about Wadesville in Andrew's car, showing him Cascade Park, the Webber's old house, the place where the orchard had been. Jonathan was polite. His eye still gleamed with a hidden excitement.

Back at my house, Andrew came to the gate. "I'm not coming out this way again. If you want to visit us that's a different matter."

"All right. I'm sorry."

He went back to the car.

"Good-bye Jonathan," I called.

"Good-bye, Uncle. Don't forget to put the bear in your will."

I saw his father rebuke him. The car drove away. I went inside and sat in the den. For the next hour I thought with regret about Marlene. Before going to bed that night I changed the sheets and pillow slips to get rid of the smell of her.

In the time between the end of examinations and the end of term Celia discovered the poetry of Yeats. She came to me full of ideas about the location of Byzantium and what the rough beast might be. I brought books from home and let her read them in class time. We knew she had done well in School

Certificate. There was no fear now of her father taking her from school. Even so, I was careful not to let her take my books home.

In the last week she came to my room with a volume of Ben Jonson's poetry. Holding it open with her finger on the page, she said, "Please, Mr. Prior, is this the poem my mother took my name from?"

## 1968–1969

The steps by which it became accepted that Celia might visit me are too minute to be properly recorded. The excuse we made was that I gave her coaching in English. Celia was sixteen. She had won her first real fight with her father and she seemed now to possess his hardness and cunning. Although Charlie still prowled his shop like a tiger there was something caged and flabby about him. He no longer gave the impression of being about to pounce. In the street we looked at each other with caution and dislike. His threat of the year before I saw now as a piece of melodrama—something to share admiration of with his daughter.

She usually visited me on a Sunday. Often we did talk about books. Her English teacher in the lower sixth was John Edgar, a crusty old sweetness-and-light man for whom English poetry had died with Robert Bridges. I tried to guide her to Eliot and Auden. She would not be guided. She jumped aimlessly, like a click-beetle: Faulkner, Pinter, Camus, Dylan Thomas, Patrick White. New Zealand poetry. Dante. Chinese poetry. She woke in me a puritanism I had not known I possessed.

"I'm sampling," she said.

To me it was more like an orgy. My own introduction to books, in Father's den, was vegetarian compared with this. I made out lists: the English novel between the wars, etc. But when I asked how she was getting on with Virginia Woolf she was likely to cry, "Oh, but I'm reading *Confessions of Zeno*. It's marvellous." With music it was the same. She skipped from Bach to Sibelius to Flamenco guitar. For three months she was in love with Mozart (man and music—an entity I refused to recognize) the way other girls were in love with Ringo Starr. A life of Mozart was the first book I let her take home to read. Even Charlie could hardly object to this. A month or two later when I found I had two copies of *Persuasion* there seemed no reason not to give her one. Again no objection from Charlie. Books, his opinion now stood, were something she'd grow out of the way Ralph had grown out of motor-bikes.

Celia laughed. "He really is wonderful. So tough and sure of himself. I mean, he's there, you can never overlook him, even when he's against things all the time. Other people shift about, you seem to be able to put your hand right through them. But not Daddy."

I was "other people". She had not been tactless, I was hypersensitive. I had come to need her affection. It seemed to run in a clear stream, the way Father's had. The slightest eddy in the current troubled me. But I kept this trouble to myself. My sight of the danger was good; as of other dangers —from her father, the town, and her impulsiveness. "You're an adult, Prior," I said, "you can keep this clean."

She asked me about her mother. "Do I look much like her at my age? It's hard to tell from photographs."

"Not much." I thought for a moment. "She was pretty. You're a *jolie laide*."

She laughed. "What a marvellous term." She repeated it with the accent that sent her French teacher into raptures. "I was scared of being pretty. I thought I was for a while. You know, insipid. But my mouth stopped it. I've got an ugly mouth, haven't I?"

I looked judicious. Her mouth was wide, faintly simian, but full rather than thin. "It reminds me of Lydia Lensky's in *The Rainbow*. An ugly beautiful muzzle." She laughed with pleasure again, but also, I thought, with a touch of derision at my turning the conversation to books. I saw her trying words under her breath. *Jolie laide*. It was going to be a defining term.

"And my poor old Mum was just pretty?"

"Not just pretty. Very pretty. In a scared sort of way. You've got the same eyes."

"Scared?"

"Without that. With a bit of your old man's glitter."

I told her how I had first seen Joyce Poole in her tennis skirt, walking down past the vineyard, a kind of temperance nymph in bacchic setting, and how she had stopped on the bridge to scratch her behind; how in my stall made of coal-sacks, from behind mounds of apples and plums, I had watched and begun to fall in love. A pretty picture, not spoiled by my satiric tone. I described the innocent progress of our affair. Celia listened in a kind of childish delight, as though to a fairy-tale. "It's like something out of a silent movie. Didn't you ever try to go to bed with her?"

"Oh yes," I said, "in the end," trying to pretend I wasn't shocked.

"What happened?"

"Nothing. We were both too inexperienced."

"Was that when you quoted Jonson at her?"

I nodded.

"Cunning old Paul."

I was offended. For a moment I thought her coarse. "Nothing of the kind. I was completely sincere. It was a very pure occasion."

Her eyes sparkled with delight. I'd become aware that my pompous turn was her favourite. Usually I could laugh at it myself. Now I got up to make a cup of tea.

"I've offended you."

"I'm all right." I went to the door. "You young people

always have to cheapen things." I'd been thrown a little off balance at finding the puppets in my story no puppets at all: they lived. I felt an ache, however slight. "Anyway, I shouldn't talk about your mother with you."

When I came back with tea she had Jonson's poems down.

> *"Come my Celia, let us prove,*
> *While we may the sports of love. . .*

I can see how it must have impressed her."

"It was the next two lines she liked."

> *"Time will not be ours for ever:*
> *He too soon our goods will sever.*

I don't think you could use this sort of thing for seducing girls today."

"There was some kind of magic," I said defensively. "The orchard—the sun. It seemed to make it appropriate." I felt closer to Joyce Poole than I had in twenty years.

Celia smiled. "I'm not cheapening it. I'm a bit envious, that's all. The last boy who wanted to sleep with me said I owed it to myself."

"Who was that?"

"The Captain of the School, no less."

I felt concern rather than jealousy. "You don't see anything in him, do you?"

"He's got nice muscles. And lots of nice teeth. Tell me about my father."

"Well, he was tough. I heard when he went into the shop with your grandfather he closed off accounts that had been allowed to stay overdue for years."

"I know all about the shop. That's where all his stories start. 'When I took over the shop from my father. . . .' He doesn't seem to have had any childhood."

So I talked about Charlie: the playground fight, the orchard raiding, the tin canoes. It was my childhood too I

130

described. But it was at once living and dead, with a kind of sepia tint; the past tense had an iron quality. I began to feel, as I had not when talking about Joyce, that I was mourning something.

"My mother didn't like your father. She thought he was leading me astray. But I was astray long before I ever met Charlie. I got rid of God when I was ten or eleven, by my own efforts. It should have been like chopping off an arm. With my brother it would have been, it would have been like tearing something out. With me—it was like clipping my finger-nails. But ever since then—I've been incomplete. I've got this sense of being hollow. I keep shifting from thing to thing. That's why I have to have a den. To stop me being completely slippery. Lightweight."

I listened to this confession with dismay. I had never questioned my identity; but nor had I made any attempt to recognize it. Why should I do it now? And in such dispirited tones? Where was that saving irony, that element that gave me weight? Celia's smile was adult. She was disappointed in me.

I grinned. "You see what indoctrination does. You're lucky your old man's an atheist."

"That means I've got nothing to reject. I've been cheated."

"Reject lack of belief. Go Roman Catholic. You'd tone in well with incense and confession."

I described a Presbyterian upbringing. Its straitness was something I had managed to forget; so now I was awed by the number of my secular choices that echoed lessons taken in those first ten years. My libertarian habits, it seemed, were Presbyterian after all, by simple inversion. Everything took its tone from Mother.

"Don't talk about it if you don't want to," Celia said.

"She knew her job."

To get away from that time I talked about Joyce Poole. My boyhood might appear in sepia tones, but the orchard and Joyce (one thing) was red and green and golden. I turned it over like an old possession.

"How did Daddy pinch her from you?"

"Is that how he describes it?"

" 'I pinched your mother from my best friend. Just moved in. Bam! Neither of them knew what had hit them.' He's so proud of himself."

"What does your mother say?"

"Just smiles. You know, dissociates herself."

"She's never told you how it happened?"

"All she says is, she was young."

"Well—it happened at the Fruitgrowers' Ball."

Celia smiled with delight. "It's another world."

"It was the day I quoted Jonson to her. She had a Spanish shawl that used to belong to her grandmother."

"I know. It's mine now."

"The hall was decorated with saddles and chain harrows and bales of hay. The band was like a sawmill." Celia laughed. "We came in—a real entrance. Paul Prior and the prettiest girl in town. Charlie had never seen her before. I was all primed up to watch him go green—no, black with envy. When he saw her it was like that." I snapped my fingers. "He came straight up the hall. Like a cannon-ball. Clean through a dance. Pushing people out of the way. And that was it. He got her. She was his."

"Just like that?"

"Just like that."

Celia laughed again. She was puzzled. "You let him take her?"

"I had no choice."

"Didn't you fight?"

"They were a force of nature."

"Oh Paul, you're pulling my leg."

"I'm not. They were made for each other. It was plain. There was nothing for me to do but stand aside."

She was still puzzled, but saw a compliment to herself: these elemental folk were her parents. Her good sense failed for a moment; she said gently, "Were you very sad?"

"Oh, I'd already decided my role was spectator. This just brought it home."

She went away with an armful of books. I had a whisky and approved of myself. Strong and silent: I would protect her from the past. Later, after another whisky, I admitted that what had moved me was an unwillingness to let Celia know I'd had a mongoloid brother.

Through that year and the beginning of the next I saw Celia almost every Sunday. We talked about Joyce and Charlie several times. These conversations in particular made me aware of the rules I was breaking. I imagined disapproval all around me. How was I getting away with it? Why didn't somebody make a move?

"It's hard to say what Mum thinks," Celia said. "She knows it's helping my schoolwork, but she knows we talk about more than that. I think she wants me to get something she missed. As for Daddy, he's decided you're too insignificant to be noticed. It's an act of will. If he stops concentrating I don't know what will happen."

My role was mixed: teacher, father, husband. I never let her see the last. Nor would I define it for myself. Books, examinations: yes, I was teacher. Ambitions: I was father, hamming the part a little for both our sakes. But in awareness of her, penetration of her (though I never more than tapped her on the hand), I was lover. It was absurd, because she was a child; yet it was understandable—she was a woman. Unlike me she was playing no role, but like me she slipped from one course to another. My awareness of her never faltered. Though she never complained I knew when her ankles were sore (she had her mother's ankles—aristocratic and treacherous). While wishing to soothe them with hands as cold as ice, I offered embrocation and quipped about the smell of the

133

football shed. I knew her eyestrain and headaches and anger at each new spot that might turn into a pimple. A faint mustiness in her breath told me when she was having her period. I knew the nights she was out with boys and believed I could tell next day how far she had let them go. All this went on behind a smiling exterior, and within a style of life I still believed cool, satiric, detached. Control, after all, was in my hands. Nothing was given or taken or lost.

Celia had her University Entrance accredited. To celebrate I risked taking her for a drive. She had lived in Wadesville all her life but had never been to a West Coast beach. I drove her out to Muriwai, where I had taken Joyce Poole twenty years earlier. She wore dark glasses and a scarf round her hair, but on that cold spring day the beach was deserted. We walked to the top of the cliffs at the south end. The view up the beach was clearer than usual. Even so the grey strip of sand dissolved at last into haze. Long green breakers slid in, a quarter of a mile apart. The scruffy sand hills, the golf course and pine plantations, seemed lower than the sea— seemed to hold it back by a kind of confidence trick.

"Can we drive along?" Celia said.

The car wheels on the wet sand made a powerful racing-car hum. We went twenty miles in just over twenty minutes, then I pulled in towards the sandhills. We walked down to the water. The world was now a saucer with us on its rim: sandhills behind, with here and there a wall of logs or wired grass to hold back the sea; in front broken water, long cold breakers, trailing spray; the strip of sand on either side, fading and vanishing. The little green car was incongruous, yet it seemed to me an emblem of courage. We walked with our legs in the water and felt it pull us seawards like something living. I began to worry about the tides. It would be a twenty mile race back to the road. I turned Celia towards the car. She had been quiet all afternoon. I asked what was worrying her.

"Nothing."

In the car she said, "You know this can never come to anything?"

I stopped with my hand on the ignition. "I like it the way it is." I waited. "Has something gone wrong?"

She was suddenly very much a child. She had no language for what she wanted to say. When she spoke her voice had a whining tone. "It's Daddy. He keeps on hanging round me."

At first I didn't understand—it was difficult to get myself out of the picture. Then I said, "How does it happen? Can you tell me?"

"I don't know. I thought I was crazy at first—it was so—slimy. But it's not my imagination. He's always—breathing on me, and looking at me, and touching me when he doesn't have to."

"Does your mother know?"

"I think so. She sees. She just gets cold and—remote."

"With you?"

"With him. With me she's kind of apologetic. But still withdrawn. It's all really her fault. She's cut herself off from him—I mean, more than just sex. She sleeps in the sunroom, but it's more than that. She thinks her life is wasted. It's so stupid—to marry a man like Daddy and expect anything more than what she got."

"So he turns to you."

"I suppose so."

"He won't even know he's doing it."

"That doesn't make it easier."

"It might even be part of this competition he's having with me. But it won't last. You'll see. He'll find a woman. It always happens. Do you think you can put up with that?"

"If it makes him happy."

"It will. And this other thing—with you. It's nothing to worry about. It's funny really. All men want to sleep with

135

their daughters. It's natural. It's one of the reasons families are so comic. All this stuff going on under the lid."

"It doesn't make me laugh." But she was more cheerful.

"Read Casanova." I quoted from memory. "How can a father truly love his daughter unless he has slept with her at least once."

"You could get fired for telling me stuff like this."

"I'm in your hands." I had shown her a stance she could take, but I wondered if there were some other. I doubted that it would work as well as mine.

We raced the tide back to the road.

"What made you say we could never come to anything?"

"I'm sorry. I was being stupid."

"No. I'd like to know."

"Well—I thought if Daddy was like that you probably would be too."

"The thought's never crossed my mind. Scout's honour."

She smiled, nodding. "We're friends."

"Friends," I agreed, feeling hollow.

"I wish my mother could be happy."

I let her out before we got into Wadesville. I saw plainly that I had been warned. Slimy, she had said. I shivered. Now I was simply teacher and friend, even in my thoughts. I promised myself. She would never have cause to use that word of me.

In January the Inveraritys stayed for three weeks at Orewa. Ralph taught Celia how to ride a surfboard. On their first Sunday at home she came to visit me, returning an armful of books. Glumly she said, "You were right about Daddy. He's got himself a girl-friend."

"How do you know?"

"He's got all manly all of a sudden. And very considerate. Holds the door open for Mum. That sort of thing. He kept saying he had to get back to see how the shop was going, and then he'd ring and say he'd stayed too late to come back."

136

She giggled. "It's awful. I have to watch his handkerchiefs for lipstick. Not that it really matters. Mum knows."

"How's she taking it?"

"Oh, pleased and hurt. Sometimes I hate parents."

The school year started and at once she was in trouble. "That bloody Inverarity girl," said Price. "She's refused to be a prefect."

"What's her reason?"

"Some nonsense. Not wanting to be a policeman." He turned to me sitting in my corner of the staffroom. "I blame you for this, Paul. Putting ideas in the girl's head."

"It's news to me," I said. "But she's right, of course. It's a lousy system."

Price threw up his hands. "See what I mean? How can I run a school. . . ? You listen, Paul, you tell that girl from me, there are going to be no special rules for her. If she won't be a prefect she'll be treated just like any other pupil. And if that means detentions with a lot of third-formers she'll just have to put up with it. I've no patience with nonconformists."

"It's time that girl was brought into line," Betty Selwyn said. "Her hair looks like a hippie's. Just because she's clever she thinks she can do as she likes."

But Celia (and the school's one or two other rebels) had support from half a dozen of us. We made a buffer between her and the staff's old guard and managed to prevent all but occasional skirmishes. Celia's hair was a shining cascade that fell to the middle of her back. At other times it was so heavy and still it seemed carved from brown wood. The reasons for Miss Selwyn's hatred of it were plain. Poor mannish career-girl Betty had convinced herself that intelligence and good looks excluded each other. Double gifts were against nature. But Celia survived the term unclipped. She came each day in her grey summer uniform, hair loose, hat perched on top. She was in my English class again and was reading and work-ing with a ferocity that alarmed me. Our friendship was cooler and more relaxed. My teaching her daily in a class of twenty-five had formalized it. I told myself this was fortunate: in this style we could go on for years, even after she'd left Wadesville College. Then she would be in her twenties and I would be only forty-five. . . . I was ruthless with that thought. See a middle-aged man in a young girl's way: gum in the eyes, body and breath stink, withered belly and stringy cock. Paul Prior in the autumn of his life lusting after spring. Slimy.

I managed to see the figure as comic.

All the same I was disappointed when Celia chose to work the May holidays in her father's shop. I had looked forward to week-day visits, and found myself thinking sourly that I hadn't learned my place.

On Sunday I read on the porch so I might see her as she came up from the hollow. The book held me. By the time her clacking sandals roused me she was almost at the gate. I jumped to my feet and cried hallo. She was carrying books as usual, and a bunch of shivery grass. Her hair was done in a plait as thick as a pick-handle. I started down the path to open the gate but she lifted the catch with her wrist and came inside.

She raised her arms and spun around. "Like it?" She was wearing an ash-grey mini-dress with long sleeves and a white Quaker collar. "I bought it with the money I'm going to earn." I thought I had never seen her looking more beautiful.

"It's marvellous. It really suits you." But I gave an inward groan.

"I wore it to please Mum. She thinks it's Sundayish."

"She's wrong."

"Shall we go inside?"

In the den she gave me the shivery grass. I thanked her and put it in a vase. It's a grass that reminds me of my mother. I used to carry bunches of it to her as a child, competing with Andrew's flowers, which a masculine sense of fitness forbade me to be seen with. "My mother was fond of this. 'God's handiwork.' " It occurred to me too that I had classified Celia's frock from Mother's chart: ash-grey. (Eggshell-blue, rust-red, clover-pink.) The naming of colours had been her one attempt at secular lyricism. "I used to pick bunches for her. And listen to little sermons on the beauty God hides away in quiet corners. Where did you get it?"

"In the hollow. It's growing at the side of the road. You don't know what you're missing, going everywhere by car. I found this too." She unfolded her handkerchief and showed me a dozen or so small greyish leaves. "I think it's some sort of herb. Not sage, but something like it. It was in the garden of the haunted house." She crushed a leaf cautiously between her teeth. "It could be something for a witches brew." Suddenly she crossed her eyes, gripped her throat. "Augh."

"What is it?"

"There are things crawling in my blood. Little snaky evil things. Augh."

"I'll get you a cup of tea." She had no histrionic talent. I was moved to see her less than perfect.

When I came back she had the leaves spread on the coffee table and was trying to identify them from *Plants of New Zealand*. "I don't think it can be a native." We searched other books and drank our tea. Then she asked for music. Instead, I put on Lorca's monologue on duende—and watched as she straightened in her chair, recognition moving in her. When the record finished she said nothing.

"Would you like to have that record?"

"I'd rather listen to it here. It wouldn't go with home." She sighed. "I'm going to Spain one day. I'm going to learn Spanish."

"There's a town called Lorca. It's hot and white and dusty." I read her several of Lorca's poems. Then she asked for flute music—something primitive. While she listened she undid her plait and shook her hair loose. She combed it with her fingers. I reflected that I had broken the first rule of den-living. I had allowed the spirit of an outsider into the room. It was haunted now, I could no longer curl up in it, foetus in womb.

The afternoon had a strange quality—as if it were shaped in an art form: reality transformed through the power of my will and imagination. It seemed to be outside time, and outside place (Wadesville); and full of conventions. Yet it was anchored to reality by the girl, who gave the impression of being able to break out of my construction whenever she should choose. She asked me what Whitmanesque meant. I took *Leaves of Grass* from the shelves and started to read *Song of Myself*. Whitman I had always considered a wind-bag. Now I found his rhetoric moving; the occasion betrayed me.

> *"Do I contradict myself?*
> *Very well then, I contradict myself.*
> *(I am large. I contain multitudes.)"*

Celia laughed. "What a marvellous licence to have. It makes him a sort of monster."

My sense of revelation darkened; became more accurate. This was myself, this multitude—horde of slippery pygmies, striking poses. If my life could be broken down it would slither away in a thousand separate directions. I closed *Leaves of Grass* and smiled at Celia. She was whole, she was bright, she glittered. A single beam, one direction. I thought foolishly that I might worship her.

"This was one of my father's favourite books." He had bought the copy I owned several weeks after my mother had burned the first one. Much of *Song of Myself* was heavily underlined. *Bravos* and *Fines* abounded. I showed Celia.

"Tell me about the poison-shed." The idea of a hoard of books in that unlikely place fascinated her. I described it again: the wind coming up through the floor, Charlie in sodden clothes, wrapping himself in sacks, then Father opening the door—Aladdin's cave. I described myself sitting there on winter afternoons reading Dickens.

"And your brother never found it?"

"He did in the end. He and my mother both knew. It gave them something else to be righteous about. Poor Andrew. There *is* a man with constipation."

She blushed. "Mum told me she met him. He looked as if he'd been wrestling with the devil."

"That's him."

"She told me about your other brother too. The mongoloid one."

I said nothing.

"How Daddy told her about him at the dance. And how she ran away and wouldn't see you again. It's different from the story you told me."

"It wasn't any of your business."

"It wasn't till years later she found out that sort of thing didn't run in families. By then Ralph and I were born. And you were in England."

"She had no right."

"Your story was nicer. Love at first sight. It really was sweet of you to make it up. But as soon as I started thinking about it I knew it couldn't be true. So I told it to Mum. You should have seen her face."

"She's a fool."

"Don't you dare talk about her like that."

I had not escaped from my shame at my loony brother. All I could think was that Celia knew—she would draw away from me.

"Anyway, if it's having a brother like that you're worried about, I already knew. Dad told me when I started coming here." She was looking at me angrily. After arguments of this sort I had found women come easily to bed. Anger tips over into desire. Relief at one surrender leads to the next. But this time I was the victim; taken by a lust so pure it gave the illusion of not being carnal. Instead of moving towards her I turned away. I took a bottle of Dry Sack from the liquor cabinet and filled two glasses. Desire passed and left me feeling as though I'd been sniffing ether. I carried one glass carefully to her across the room.

"Here you are. Produce of Spain. We'll drink to Lorca."

She took up the new tone without a pause. The brief quarrel had shaken her and her hand trembled as she reached for the glass. But she smiled and said, "Real sherry. I've never tasted it." It pleased me to see how eagerness for something new, greed even, pushed out her other emotions. She sipped. "It tastes like raisins."

"To the memory of Lorca."

"Is he dead?"

"He disappeared in the civil war. Franco's boys probably got him."

Her eyes filled with tears—the surrender, I could not help thinking, that in an older woman would have taken us to the bedroom. We drank our sherry and after a while she said, "Thank you for trying to make it romantic for me."

I did not understand.

"Dad and Mum. But I like the true story best." She smiled. "It's in character."

We talked for another half hour. Then it was time for her to go. She asked to borrow Whitman; and picked up a copy of *Memoirs and Confessions of a Justified Sinner* I'd bought a few days earlier.

"What's this like?"

"Good. Take it if you like. It's got a Wadesville flavour."

Going down the path, I said, "You'd better buy some chewing-gum in town. Get that sherry off your breath."

"Who cares what people think?"

"Charlie Inverarity isn't people."

"I can handle him."

I wondered if the sherry had made her a little drunk. "Are you all right? I can run you home."

"No. I want to walk."

I opened the gate and let her out.

"Have fun in the shop."

"Ugh." But her mood had changed again. She kept her hand on the gate, then suddenly leaned over it and kissed my cheek. "Thank you for being so nice to me."

She walked off down the road towards the hollow.

## May 16, 1969

I arrived in Takapuna with no idea how to fill the afternoon.
The last thing I wanted was to be caught by Penny, who
would break the week into pieces and put it together again
like a jigsaw puzzle. I drove to the furniture factory, a long
low fibrolite building grafted on to an older brick and plaster
one. Andrew's office is on a mezzanine floor. It had always
struck me as being like something offered on a tray, under a
glass dish. He sits behind glass, cut off by glass from his
secretary, and looks out over the upholstery room (a "room"
as large as a school assembly hall). I climbed the stairs and
stopped outside the office. The secretary saw me and
beckoned me in. "He won't be long. He's on the phone."
Andrew was talking earnestly, but his eyes stopped on me
with a questioning look. I shook my head—nothing serious
—and turned to watch the men working. *Priors* makes ugly
furniture. Sofas were on the near end of the floor, like quilted
sarcophagi, and pink porky chairs on the far end. I thought
I'd almost as soon be in munitions.

"Come in, Paul."

He had a plain brown desk with a wooden chair behind it.
The customer's chair was upholstered. I sat down. Andrew
was without his usual calm.

"I've been looking into this question of a retail shop. It's
a tricky business."

I nodded.

144

"I'd like to get your views some time."

"I've got no views. It just surprises me that stuff out there sells at all."

"Of course it sells. You don't know the market."

"I don't want to know the market."

So, in ten seconds, we were glaring at each other. My glare was weak—a thing of habit only. I closed my eyes. "But I didn't come to talk about that."

"What did you come to talk about?"

"I don't know."

"Why don't you go down home and have a rest? Penny'll make you a cup of tea."

"I will soon."

He pushed some papers to one side, then brought them back again. "Have the police been bothering you?"

"Not much. No more than they have to."

"Are they any closer to catching the man?"

"I suppose they must be. They've got enough people working on it."

"What line are they taking? Any likely suspects?" Normally he would be stuffy about a thing like this: the "seamy side" was best ignored.

"The car's all they've got. A green Mini like mine."

He drew back suddenly; sharpened his eyes: his pulpit look. "Why did you have to get mixed up in it?"

"I didn't exactly——"

"Your whole life's a mess, Paul. Nothing but self-indulgence and pleasure. Women, drink, the stuff you call art. No discipline, no belief, no order. It's as if our mother had never existed."

"Listen——"

"Everything went overboard. You gave in to every appetite you ever had. It's no wonder to me you've ended like this."

"I haven't ended." Celia had ended. "Anyhow, I didn't

come for a sermon. There's a girl dead. Nothing changes that."

"She's in merciful hands."

Oh my God, I thought, here it is again. The image I always had when he talked of God was of our old black dunny with wetas on the ceiling and a candle in a chipped enamel holder. I was fond of it—I could afford to laugh: such a joke, such an antique. But the glimpse I caught now was obscene. I got up from my chair and went out of my brother's office. Like him I had a nose for poisoned air. I drove down to the beach and sat looking over the water. Soon I felt less sick and started to work up a rage. That cretin, I thought, that half-man, that self-castrated, mother-worshipping, obscurantist, priestly, wowser prick. What a mind! What an oily little mess of cogs and bearings! Press the button and out came the card. *God in His infinite wisdom has called this sinner to the judgement seat.* I got out of the car and spat.

Then I walked on the beach, trying to think of Celia. But Celia was far away. Transubstantiated. Ashes.

The motion of the sea began to soothe me. Black-backed gulls waddled out of my path. The salty, savoury smell of rotting seaweed came to my nostrils and made me think of the fish soup, and seaweed soup, Mother had fed us at the kitchen table. "Eat it up, it's good for you." Andrew, to please her, asked for more.

I passed his house and glimpsed Penny busy in her kitchen. Patient Penelope, I thought, her husband was under a worse spell than Circe's. I turned my head to the sea and went on.

"Paul." A thin seagull cry. I was far enough away to pretend I hadn't heard. Conversation with Penny was like a walk in a formal garden: gravelled path, staked and labelled shrub, dwarf, common exotic. Never a weed. "Paul." I would have enough of her in the evening. But for people like Penny I find myself experiencing a kind of rudimentary social concern; a sense that a wrong response might bring a whole

146

card-house of verities tumbling down. I usually smile and do what's expected of me, meanwhile building up ill-humour to be taken out on class or car or washing-machine. "Paul." I turned, acting puzzlement; then walked back along the sand.

"I thought I'd get a bit of sea air."

"Paul, if you're going that way would you look for Jonathan?"

I'd forgotten the boy was on holiday.

"He went off this morning for a walk round the rocks and all he took was an orange. He'll be starving by now. Tell him to come home for lunch."

I looked at my watch and Penny said quickly, "Yes, I know, it's late." She was not a maker of pleas or confessions, but suddenly she said, "Paul, will you talk to him? He's acting so strangely—as though he's——" She struggled, "—in a different world—behind a glass wall." This was not what she wanted; she shrugged impatiently. "He just mopes off by himself. He won't talk or eat. He just goes for walks or goes to bed."

Why do I always think of sex? I had Jonathan's trouble diagnosed before Penny had properly begun. Guilt. Presbyterian dong-beater's guilt. A dread disease. A killer. It had helped cripple the boy's father. Now it returned—a visiting sin.

"Has Andrew talked to him?"

"Andrew's useless. Besides, he doesn't know. He only sees what it suits him to see."

I looked at her in surprise. It was the first critical judgement I had known her pass on Andrew. Although it pleased me I wasn't going to be drawn. "It's probably nothing. Probably some worry at school. I'll talk to him."

"Thank you, Paul. I'd be so grateful. And don't tell Andrew."

I walked along the beach again. Poor Jonathan. Poor little bugger. His father smelled of moral disgust the way other men smell of after-shave lotion. The boy must have caught a whiff every time he'd gone near. But I had thought he was tough, I'd thought he'd survive—like me? My father was different. His deepest need was of privacy—and privacy was the gift he offered us, while our mother offered love, precepts, a Path: bondage. That he was more selfish than she, and lazier, seemed unimportant to me. I kept my eyes on the damage.

Round the first headland I found Jonathan sitting on a rock peeling an orange. He was trying to get the skin off in one piece—a sign, I thought, that he wasn't wholly submerged. I sat down beside him. "You could fill that up with sand and leave it on the beach. Someone would think they'd found a real orange."

He gave me a faint smile. He obviously thought the idea cheap. "Have you seen my father?"

"Yes. And your mother. She's worried about your lunch."

"I bought a pie." He split the orange and offered me half. There was a tension in him, unfurtive, that suggested fear and lostness rather than guilt. I wondered if I'd been wrong in my guess at his trouble.

"What was Dad like?"

"All right. Normal." I waited. "Have you got some trouble with him?"

"No." He said nothing more for several minutes, and I said nothing. His tension had reached out to me. Absolutely still, he thought something out. Then he started eating pieces of orange.

"Have they caught the man who killed that girl?"

I shook my head.

"Do you think they will?"

"Yes. It's only a matter of time."

"What was she like?"

"Nice. A nice girl."

"Why would someone want to kill her?"

148

"I don't know, Jonathan. Probably he doesn't know himself. A fit of insanity. Something like that."

"You mean he was mad?"

"He must have been. He might even have done it in a kind of blank. That happens sometimes. Or people hear a voice telling them to kill."

"From God?"

"Usually. At least, that's what they think."

"I don't believe in God."

"No?" It did not seem strange. "Nor do I."

Jonathan finished his orange. I remembered my piece and ate it. I did not think religion—loss of belief—was his trouble; or, as had seemed likely for a moment, that my connection with Celia had brought him to a realization of death.

"How do people get mad?"

"There's no one way. All sorts of pressures—delusions."

"Voices from God?"

"Not only that. Hundreds of ways."

He was quiet for a moment. "But why that girl?"

"Chance," I said, "chance." It was the way he seemed to weigh even this that made me understand at last that he was bringing himself to tell me something he knew about the murder.

"What is it, Jonathan?"

He pulled a kind of tragic clown's face—the sort of thing that must until then have been a game with him. It kept him, I think, from crying.

"Can I show you something?"

The walk along the beach was like an episode in a cheap movie—the finding of the body in the wardrobe. Thinking of it now I hear music in crescendo. Jonathan led me to the boat-shed on the front of Andrew's section. The building hid us from Penny in the house. He took a rusty key from his pocket and unlocked the padlock on the door. Inside, on its trolley, was the old cabin cruiser Andrew had bought with the house. Jonathan squeezed along the side of it and levered himself up until he could climb into the cabin. He opened the door to the engine and felt inside. I saw him shifting things carefully. Then he came back—over the side, along the narrow gap—and handed me a newspaper parcel.

As I unwrapped it he pressed himself against my side. He gave way to horror and grief: responsibility was mine. He wept against my shoulder. I kept my actions slow: unwrapped the paper, dropped it, handled the books as though I were in a second-hand bookshop. *Leaves of Grass*, with the name Henry Prior on the fly-leaf. *Memoirs and Confessions of a Justified Sinner*. I had moved into a world where things were recognizable only physically. I put my arm round Jonathan and let him cry.

"Your father?"

"He's the only one with another key."

"Andrew."

My feelings take no shape—I remember them simply as an amorphous lump in which horror, comprehension, incomprehension, all had a part. Everything else has clarity. There were grains of sand at the roots of Jonathan's hair. His breath and his tears were warm on the side of my neck. A yellow surf-board with a black stripe running down it just off centre leaned against the wall of the shed. I remember thinking, Mondrian, and giving an almost terrified yelp at the inconsequence of the thought. I looked at the books again. *Leaves of Grass* had foxing on the title page. A hair that must have been Celia's protruded like a book-mark from *Song of Myself*. I held it between my fingers for a moment, then dropped it to the floor of the shed.

Jonathan moved away from me. He wiped his arm across his eyes. "What are we going to do?" he said.

"Talk. We've got to talk."

"He must have——"

"Not here." I picked up the paper and wrapped it round

the books. "Put them back. Exactly where you found them."

He obeyed almost eagerly: along the side of the boat, into the cabin; then back to my side.

"My car's parked at the boat-ramp. Do you think you can get there without your mother seeing?"

"Yes."

"Off you go then."

He slipped out, looked around for a second, then crouched and ran. Andrew, I thought, you've really done it this time. I locked the shed. I went back along the beach, up a right-of-way, and walked through the streets to my car. Jonathan was waiting inside.

"Can we go somewhere else?"

I drove to Milford and parked at the beach. His story came in a rush. On Sunday afternoon his mother had taken the Rover to call on her parents. Later Andrew had borrowed a neighbour's car to visit his factory foreman, who was sick. The neighbour, Mrs. Tillotson, was a widow, sixty-five and partly blind. She kept the green Mini as a kind of memorial to her husband. Andrew took her for drives in it now and then and borrowed it on a strict system: one charity drive earned one loan.

On Sunday he drove away, saying he'd be gone for a couple of hours. At once Jonathan fetched a key his father thought lost and got his surf-board from the boat-shed. (Andrew had locked it up at the end of March, which for him was the end of summer.) He surfed for an hour, then waxed the board and put it away in the exact position he'd taken it from. His mother came home at four and his father at quarter-past six. Penny asked Andrew what had made him late and he said he'd gone from the foreman's place to talk some Session business with Peter Bax.

On Tuesday morning while Penny was shopping Jonathan decided to risk another hour with his surf-board. The waves were running—other boys were out. He went to the shed, and saw that someone had shifted the board several feet. At once he was alert. Was his father setting a trap? He poked around, looking for clues.

"I didn't believe at first it was him. I thought he must have been protecting you, or something." He wept again: that time must have seemed long ago.

I put my arm around him. "Leave it all to me now. Forget about it if you can." (Kindly old Uncle Paul! Forget your father strangled a girl.)

We drove around the North Shore for the rest of the afternoon. Alternately the boy wept and talked. Questions. Why? Why did he do it? What's going to happen? I too asked myself, why? how?—and seemed on the point of understanding, but could not take the final step. It was like trying to remember a name that eludes, or picture a face known in childhood. But I had a dozen plans. I would take Jonathan with me—run. We'd leave the mess to sort itself out. Or: I'd call the police—they could pick Andrew up at the factory. None of us need ever see him again. Or: I'd get the books—burn them—steal the car. . . . Or: I'd take Andrew into the bush, shoot him, bury the body.

"What are you going to do?"

"I'll tell him he's got to see me in the morning. . . . I'll have a plan by then."

"What plan?"

"I don't know. One that's best for you and your mother. Do you think you can get through the night?"

"What if he finds out I know?"

"He won't hurt you. He won't hurt his family."

"But what if he finds out?"

"He won't. There's no way he can. . . . You go to bed early. Say you don't feel well."

I took him to a public lavatory where he washed his face and combed his hair. Then we went home. It was nearly five o'clock. Jonathan went straight to his room.

"It's all right," I said to Penny. "It's school trouble, like I thought. They're a wet bunch of teachers at that place." I improvised a tale of minor persecutions. "I've told him how to handle it. He's a sensible boy. He'll be all right."

"Don't tell Andrew," Penny said.

We had a cup of tea and talked about the boy. His father was giving him a rough time. Penny saw her "golden mean" in danger.

"I believe in discipline. Strictness. But he won't allow him any freedom at all. He's got it all laid down in do's and don'ts. Like a sort of chart. It's too rigid." Order, she was seeing, had its dangers. I said nothing, but let her run on. She was, I thought, so much a nonentity she became memorable. A monster of ordinariness. How had she got through the week with a husband who'd murdered a girl? Had there been no sign—*nothing* strange? Terror in the dark, remorse? —signal across the gulf between his blue-sheeted bed and her pink one? And before the murder? There were years of hatred in him—building up. There must have been. She'd lived with him seventeen years. Why hadn't she seen it? Warned somebody?

Finally: She was there—available. Why hadn't he strangled her?

Andrew came home at half-past five. I found I couldn't control myself. My bowels were suddenly loose and my eyes running. I went to the lavatory, where I made a noise like one of my father's specials. At the other end of the house somebody closed a door.

When I went back to the kitchen (like Jonathan, with washed face and combed hair) Andrew was drinking tea and reading the newspaper.

"There you are, Paul. Seen this?"

I shook my head.

"There's not much news. Comfort House have got a new lounge suite. See." He tried to show me a full-page ad. "It's a bit like our new line. We've got them beaten on price though."

"You men move out of here," Penny said.

We went into the sitting-room. Andrew sat in a *Priors* chair and turned the pages of his paper. Above his head a formation of china ducks headed for the space-heater. I looked out the windows at the beach. A boy in a wet-suit was riding miniature waves.

"There's nothing new in the murder case. 'Investigations continuing. . . .' I suppose that's a way of saying they're stuck."

"Yes."

"It looks as if he might get away. Well, the sooner it's forgotten the better." He turned a page; made an exclamation of disgust. "Look. A disgrace." His finger was on a photograph of a newly-opened church. "It's like a cowshed. The government shouldn't have let Mormons into the country in the first place."

A few moments later Penny called us for dinner. I went to Jonathan's bedroom. He was lying face down on the bed.

"Are you all right?"

"Yes."

"It's tea time. Do you think you can manage?"

He followed me back to the dining-room and sat down in his place.

Penny had cooked steak—"Paul's favourite meal." But she had done it to suit Andrew: fried every drop of juice out. He ate in his usual fashion, ignoring as far as he could what was on his plate. Eating was a necessary chore. Nevertheless his mood was, for him, expansive. Nodding at me, he said, "I'm glad to see you've shaved those things off your face. Now if you get a barber on to your hair you'll start to look like a civilized person again."

I looked at his hands. They were white, strong, hairless. Nails as pink as candy. Very deft with knife and fork, cutting uniform squares of steak. These were the hands, merciful hands, that had strangled Celia and tried to rip the hair from her head. I tried to picture the scene. An exercise in horror—purely cerebral. I had no realization of it. My concern was for the boy. He had spoken the grace evenly enough, but his first forkful of meat was still in his mouth. He couldn't swallow.

His mother too had noticed. In a moment she said, "Try to eat, Jonathan. Steak's good for you."

"I'm not really hungry."

"Again?" Andrew said. "What's wrong with the boy?"

"He'll eat something. Won't you, Jonathan?"

"He'd better. I don't pay good money for food just to have him turn his nose up at it."

"My stomach feels funny."

I tried to help. "Maybe it's that pie."

"Pie? Jonathan?"

"I had one for lunch."

"Pie?" Andrew chimed in. His indignation was moral: pies came from the underworld. Jonathan stared at him. There was a bruised look about his face. Suddenly he put his mouth down and dropped chewed meat in his hand.

"Go to your room," Andrew cried. His voice was too light to be patriarchal. "I'll come and see you later."

The boy ran.

"My apologies, Paul. That sort of thing doesn't usually happen at my table."

We ate the rest of the meal without talking. As soon as it was over Penny went to Jonathan's room. When she came back she said, "You're not to touch him, Andrew. He has got an upset stomach. If he's no better in the morning I'm getting the doctor." Her defiance took in me: so much for my cure.

"You pamper him," Andrew said.

We drank tea again, then Penny set herself to mend the

155

evening. Bright, formal chatter: she had the gift. I had only to nod and smile. Later Andrew fetched his satchel and laid papers on the coffee table: the rough plans of a retail shop. I looked at my watch and saw it was half-past eight.

"Not now, Andrew. Come across to my place in the morning."

"I can't do that." He looked as if I'd insulted him. "It's a working day. What's wrong with now?"

"A social occasion." I managed to smile at Penny. "Besides, I've got to go. There's someone I've got to see."

"Well, I'm not coming to Wadesville. You're on holiday. You come and see me." He pointed his finger at my chest. "It's your money I'm working for."

"I'm taking my money out."

"What?"

"I'm taking my money. Out of the business."

"You can't."

"Why not? It's mine."

"It's not yours. It's the company's."

"All right. I'll sell." I had the deception going nicely now. "But I'm not talking about it tonight. Not in front of Penny. You come to my place. Tomorrow morning. Early."

"Listen, Paul——"

"Tomorrow."

"You're crazy."

"Do you mind if I use the bathroom?"

I threw water on my face; wondering if my talent for improvisation would be adequate for the morning. It would be too much to expect. Plans were needed. A plan. *The* plan. The large and immovable thing I could push Andrew behind so no one need ever see him again.

Back in the hall, I opened Jonathan's bedroom door. A movement came from the bed.

"All right?"

"Yes."

"I'm going now."

"Yes."

"He's coming in the morning. He thinks it's about business."

The boy said nothing.

"Good night."

"Good night."

"Try to sleep."

"I will."

I had the feeling I was deserting him. "He won't come in here. Your mother told him you were sick."

"Yes." His voice was remote—he had begun to ride some fantasy; escape. I hoped it would last until he was asleep. I closed the door and went back to the living-room.

"Paul," Penny said firmly, "I think you should sit down and talk this out now. It's always best that way." She stood up. "I'll leave you men together."

"No, Penny. I'm going home." I moved to the door. "Tomorrow morning, Andrew." His face had taken a strained, embittered look—as in our mother anger made him yellow. I felt a kind of forlorn pleasure.

"Paul, I've worked like a slave for you. . . ."

I drove across the harbour bridge and nosed out through Herne Bay, Avondale, New Lynn, blindly as a mole. I drove past Waikumete cemetery and the crematorium into a territory I had learned through the soles of my feet. Wadesville—winy, puritan. The words moved calmly across my mind as though fellowship between them could not be more natural. I stopped the car at the roadside and looked down at the town. The lights were a luminous skeleton. The flesh I saw was that of Wadesville thirty years ago. My Wadesville. Andrew's? How had Andrew been made? I could no more explain him than I could the town. Nor could I think about him. I could only watch what my mind supplied: the boy in the kitchen, blacking Mother's stove; in the orchard, searching for eggs; behind the teller's grille; running with the jar of pears. The boy crying without shame, turning in the circle as the caps flicked out. The man, running. There was no change in the working of my mind as it moved into the future. It seemed that memory supplied these images too: Andrew running, hands held out; Andrew dead, face down in the bracken; Andrew sinking, weighted with stones, his face withdrawing like a fish into the dark green water. An event floated up, ready-made, with a shape I could not question. I handled it, opened it like a book. It filled me with dread, yet, as had my losing Joyce Poole, it gave me pleasure.

*The* plan. It was *done*. I sat there longer, until my mind was able to work on it. And longer still.

Lights were going out in the town as I started the car and drove down the hill towards home. I turned along Farm Road. To Celia I said, "Leave it to me." And to Jonathan sleeping on the North Shore, "Leave it to Uncle Paul."

Then, inside the house, I saw that Charlie had paid another visit. I looked at the wreck of the den with a sense of *déjà vu*. In the middle of the floor books with their covers ripped off were heaped as though for a bonfire. The pictures lay on top of them, kicked full of holes or bent like pieces of tin. The record-player was chopped in pieces and the records smashed. There was no whole piece of glass or pottery in the room. Celia's shivery grass was emptied on top of the pile of books. Henry Bear lay beside it, split down the middle. His insides were the colour of butter.

A sack flapped in the window Charlie had climbed through. The tomahawk lay in my chair. I lifted it out and sat down.

"Fair enough, Charlie," I said.

## May 17, 1969

It was seven o'clock when I woke in my chair. The sacks breathed heavily. In time with them the light increased and faded. The ruined den seemed ancient, fallen into natural decay, and I an intruder with a curiosity merely scientific. These broken artefacts, torn books, spoke of a past whose connection with myself could not be traced. This was the day of the plan. I had come out of the world I'd locked myself in as my idiot brother died, into the world where my brother Andrew's death was taking place. This I must attend.

The tomahawk had lain across my thighs all night. I stood up and dropped it on the heap of books. I crossed the room to the calendar—the only thing Charlie had not torn down. Egmont, touched with sunlight, stood above a dark sea and dark land. "At 5 a.m. saw for a few Minutes the Top of the peaked Mountain above the Clowds . . . it is of a prodigious height and its top is covered with everlasting snow. . . ." I pulled the calendar down and tore it across, halving the mountain and eighteenth-century map. Past and future were irrelevant.

But the word "prodigious" echoed in my mind. She had used it of Mozart, her father, George Eliot; of a weta, a tree, the heat of the sun: like me at sixteen, tasting words, careless of meaning, liking above meaning the shape of them and the feel of them on the tongue. I was desperate to feel grief for her, but all I could feel was anger at the waste of a life so full of promise. Victim of a madman—my second loony brother. Better if she had been struck by lightning. One could at least have understood the laws involved. Andrew was outside the universe of laws, in some place where blood was water. His life too was destroyed, he was victim as much as she—but I had no conviction of this, I could feel nothing for him, not even mild pity. I simply knew my job: to "carry" him again a little way.

I knew I had an hour. He started work at eight o'clock and would make a point of reaching my place at that time. I showered and had a shave. For the first time in years I took little notice of my face in the mirror.

Then I had a breakfast of coffee and toast. There were twenty minutes left. I went outside and walked in the wilderness behind the house. My ewes jumped at the sight of me and hurried into an angle of the fence. They watched me sidelong with their yellow eyes. It was another cold morning. The wind flapped my shirts and underclothes on the line. They had been there since Sunday morning. I looked at the briefs with distaste. Sexy. So one of my girl-friends had told me. Also, she insisted, that tight little pouch killed sperm at first base, by overheating. I was, she had said, a spermicidal maniac. I frowned and averted my eyes.

The ewes went deeper into the corner. Their grey wool snagged on the barbs of the fence. I supposed they would find grazing on the section if by some chance that part of the plan failed that had me survive. Someone would come to take them away. They were so elderly it would probably be to the works. I told them not to worry—swimming was one of the half dozen things I did well. On the farm the Herefords were grazing by the water trough. Their breath steamed lightly and their flanks shone in the weak morning sunlight. Their days were definitely numbered, but that could not be laid at my door—unless as an eater of meat I must take responsibility. For ten minutes I found refuge in trivialities.

Then I could not keep from looking every moment at my watch.

At a minute to eight Andrew's black Rover came into sight and cruised down into the hollow. I heard a gear-change at the tight corner. A moment later the car came up and rolled in its English way along to my house. Andrew sat like a chauffeur: straight back, two hands on the wheel. He turned the car to face the way it had come. I had thought once, with my usual cleverness where he was concerned, that the noises of the Rover suited him perfectly: the murmuring of the well-bred engine, the discreet cough of the closing door. Standing on the small concrete yard outside the kitchen, with my shirts clapping in a friendly way at my back, I heard the sounds again. They found no point of reference in my mind. The gate gave a secretive squeak. Footsteps sounded on the path with the measure of good-mannered chewing. I tried to cling to an apprehension of him—the man of no appetites, man of disapprovals. I tried to imagine him eyeing my unweeded path. But his feet on the porch, his knuckles on the door, set me drifting again. With hysteric levity I thought, who's that knocking on my door?

I gave myself a moment. Why not? A last self-indulgence. I gave myself until he should knock again.

"Paul," he yelled in an angry voice. He thought I was still in bed. In a moment he banged heavily on the frame of my bedroom window.

All right, I said, here we go.

I went through the house and pulled back the heavy front door. He was immediately in front of me, with his hand raised to strike the door with its heel.

"Hello, Andrew," I said.

"What's been going on here?" He stepped back to glare at sacks on the windows. "Didn't you hear me knocking?"

"I was in the back yard." I left him to close the door and led the way to the den. "Sit down if you can find a place."

He looked at the ruined room with an expression of outrage.

"What happened here?"

"I had a visit from Charlie Inverarity."

"He did this? You let him?"

"It happened while I was out."

"But this is—criminal. This is valuable property." His eyes were on the record-player. "Have you called the police?"

"No."

"But why not? You can't let him get away with a thing like this."

"He was upset about his daughter."

"That's preposterous. What's his daughter got to do with it? This is—criminal."

"Sit down, Andrew."

"I'll do no such thing. Not until you've telephoned the police."

"Sit down." I put my hand on his chest and pushed. He went back into my chair so hard that he bounced a little way forward off its back. Before he could get up I said, "If I call the police it's you they'll arrest, not Charlie."

"What?" There was an unnatural quickness in the forward dart of his head. He understood. Before I was properly aware of having taken the first step, he had gone the whole way and seen what he must do. "You'd better explain that remark."

"All right." I sat down facing him. For a moment I suffered a kind of thinning of consciousness so that my brother seemed to have no substance—a flat shape on a flat surface. "You killed Celia Inverarity."

He looked at me steadily; and now he was solid again: Andrew the deskman, Presbyterian elder. I wondered if I were mad. He said, "You're mad, Paul. You've finally——" he gave a small laugh, "—flipped." The word brought me to myself. Andrew using slang? This wasn't Andrew, this was somebody else.

"Tell me how you did it."

He stood up. "That stuff about taking your money out—that was a trick to get me over here."

I nodded.

"A lie." He began to walk to the door. "See a doctor, Paul." He stopped and waved disgustedly at the room. "It's the sort of life you lead. But I wash my hands of it. You're on your own now. Heaven knows, I tried."

"Sit down, Andrew."

"I'm going to work."

"You'll find the police waiting if you do."

"Meaning what? You'll ring them?"

"As soon as you go out the door."

"And what will you say?"

"I'll tell them about your neighbour's car. Did you wipe it, Andrew? Did you wipe Celia's finger-prints off?"

"All right." He came back from the door and sat in the chair. He looked at me with dislike. "What do you propose to do?"

That's it, I thought, the confession. As simple as that. I almost broke down. I must have hoped until that moment, secretly from myself, that he would be able to prove himself innocent—bring out some humourless Andrewism. Smile his condescending smile. The hope was lost in the instant I became aware of it. I began to shout. Why? For God's sake why? What had made him do it? He sat impassive under this, with a stony, inviolate expression that enraged me.

"I know," I cried, "I can read you. You saw her coming up the road and your cock started to twitch. You've never had a girl, have you? Not a real one. Only that frigid bag of a wife."

He straightened in the chair. "How dare you?"

"What did you do, Andrew? Get her in the car and ask her to feel how big it was? And strangle her when she wouldn't? Or maybe you had to kill her to make yourself feel clean again after all those dirty thoughts." I went on for some time, past

the point at which he might have answered with a similar kind
f raving. He drew back from this, far back to the outer
reaches of his ground, and made himself inviolate again.
Unshakeable.

Quietly he said, "You're rotten, Paul. Absolutely rotten.
You poison everything you touch. There's not a single thing
that's good and decent—and holy, that you haven't tried to
pour filth on. You corrupt everything. Even my son. You've
tried to corrupt even him. You're not coming into my house
again. I'm going to see to that. I'm not having you anywhere
near my family. Or Mother. I'm the one who loves her. I'm
the one who keeps her alive."

It was no trouble to get him to talk after that. The trouble
would have been to make him stop. He showed me his childhood; and his adolescence—a kind of torture chamber where
his human nature racked him and our mother stood Christ-
like, with blessing and forgiveness, if he could only reach her.

"I had to make up for you, did you know that? And
Father. And John. I had to be all of you. There were times
when I was so—unworthy, I felt if I went near her and she
touched me she'd get sick and die."

That was his education. The other things in the long run
never counted. I was listening with an awe that was close to
fear; a knowledge forming in me that I would be asked to pay
for hearing these things. He was talking easily, in a way that
was mildly humorous, even critical. The central truths were
not in question.

I asked about the factory, money.

"The factory was my reward."

A diagram of his universe might be made of two over-
lapping circles, the perimeter of each enclosing the centre of
the other. In one circle things of the spirit: a stern God, a
merciful Christ, and Mother, combining these attributes (a
kind of Holy Ghost). In the other: bank account, house, car
—Paul Prior squeaking at the outer rim, so distant his certain

164

damnation could be ignored. Andrew lived in the common ground, untroubled, until I came back.

I forced a battle on him. When we were face to face he found his certainties shaken. And as I brought weapons from one rim, so he was forced to seek his at the other. He left his safe middle ground for the haunted territory, and there, at last, a call reached him for blood. (These are my words. I reject their apocalyptic tone. He believed he was chosen, but the truth is much less simple. The whole of his life overflowed into the killing.)

"How did you kill her?" I asked.

Sunday the twelfth of May was a Sunday like any other. Visiting the sick gave Andrew pleasure only as a duty accomplished. He borrowed the car key from Mrs. Tillotson and set off for Birkenhead, where his upholstery foreman nursed a case of stomach flu. He did not expect to be welcome, or to stay long.

The foreman's wife took him at first for a doorstep evangelist. Then, flustered, confessed that her husband was out playing golf. His flu had got better overnight—it was almost a miracle. Andrew drove away angrily. If it had not been Sunday he would have gone straight to the office and worked. Instead he drove north. As was usual when he met dishonesty, he called our mother to his side. At the top of the Albany hill he (they) stopped in a parking-bay and looked across the upper harbour to the Wadesville valley. It appeared to lie under a brown industrial smog. (Things, on that day, had a way of confirming his view; isolating him.)

"Look what they've done to our home, Mother."

The drive that followed, around the top of the harbour, through Riverhead and down the motorway, was a kind of Orphean descent. The Wadesville of his imagination was changeless: old wooden house, orchard, garden, kitchen with roaring stove and singing kettle; mother, Goddess of

the Hearth—Andrew, wise child, acolyte. He came down
that day into a town of hoardings, shops, traffic lights, where
Sunday motor-bike gangs clustered outside milkbars and
girls in jeans and leather mini-skirts stood on the corners
with jaws moving on cuds of gum. This was no longer
Wadesville. This was the town of Paul Prior. He drove
through it and turned into Farm Road. At the top of the hill
he stopped and looked across the valley. In place of the house
and orchard stood giant fibrolite storage sheds. Beside them
the dead creek ran. He walked from the car to the edge of the
hill and looked down at my house; and me on the sunny
porch, reading a book. He watched me turn one page; two;
dig in my ear for wax and wipe my finger on the leg of my
trousers.

A girl went by, carrying books. He saw her instantly as
mine. A law began to operate. The three of us, and Mother,
were in a valley outside common nature, where other beings
were insubstantial as ghosts. Only we were real. He watched
the girl walk down the hill. Everything brought a shock of
recognition. Books, plaited hair, bare legs, religious collar.
The girl went out of sight. He glimpsed her a little while later
moving in the scrub, where she seemed to be picking something. On the veranda I moved my book out of the sun. The
girl came on to the road again and set off along its edge,
carrying a bunch of grass. He watched our meeting on the
path and saw her spin like a dancer to show off her dress. We
went inside.

Insult had given place to a sense of defilement. He waited.
At the end of an hour he drove to Cascade Park. Here he had
picnicked with mother, and swung on swings while she
watched to see that he didn't go too high. Bracken and scrub
covered the playing ground now. The sound of the falls was
thinner than it had been in his childhood. He walked down
to the creek and came back on a path through the scrub. He
was inspecting the place, like a man in an empty house. The

tiny universe peopled by Mother, himself, the girl, me, widened to include it.

He drove back to the hill. It never occurred to him that Celia might have left. He watched the house. He had the sense of being about to perform some important action, some cleansing action, but no knowledge yet of what it might be. It touched Mother, he knew. And me. With wonder he found that his love for her included me.

Celia came on to the veranda. She put up a hand to shield her eyes from the sun. He saw that her hair was unplaited. At the gate she kissed my cheek. He looked at me sadly, with forgiveness. The girl was evil: an agent. She walked along the road towards the hollow. (A car went by in a world governed by other laws.) He saw her wave, me wave in return, and she went out of sight into the hollow. Andrew ran his car to the edge of the road and faced it the way the girl was walking. She came up between the banks of dusty scrub, shielding her eyes again. She was smiling and her face was flushed. He noticed that a button of her collar was undone.

"Excuse me," he said. "Can I give you a ride?"

"Oh." She was startled. He, for her, had been in another world. "No. No thank you. I like walking." She kept on.

"I'm Paul Prior's brother."

She stopped and faced him.

"I was on my way to see Paul. But it's a bit late now. Can I give you a lift back down the road?"

"Well. . . ." There was no way out. "As far as town would help. I'll walk from there." She went round to the passenger's side and got in the car. "How did you know I was a friend of his?"

"I stopped to have a look at the view. I saw you come out."

She blushed. He had a sense of having begun her defeat. He waited to start the car until she had settled herself. She had to prop herself up a little, bracing her back on the back of the seat, to pull her skirt under her thighs. Then she smoothed it on top and held the books in her lap.

"What's your name?"

"Celia Inverarity."

Everything had a place in the pattern: her loose hair, dress, naked legs. Now her name.

"Are you any relation of Charlie Inverarity?"

"He's my father." She looked suddenly at him. "Do you know him?" He smelled wine on her breath.

"I knew him when we were boys. He was Paul's friend."

"Yes. Paul coaches me English. I go to the school he teaches at."

Andrew started the car and drove towards Wadesville. He felt no pity for the girl.

"I see he lends you books."

"Yes."

"What are they?"

"*The Private Memoirs and Confessions of a Justified Sinner.* That's by James Hogg. Paul says it's good."

"What's the other one?"

It was lying on top. She flicked the cover open. "*Leaves of Grass.* It's poetry."

Andrew saw Father's name on the fly-leaf. This was the book he had picked up from the sideboard when he was seven years old. Laboriously he had read out the name. "Let me see that," said Mother. For several minutes she had turned pages. Then she opened the door of the stove and pushed it into the flames. "That's the only way to deal with filth."

The same book, with Father's name. It was a sign, and Mother an example. He turned the car into the road to Cascade Park.

"That's the wrong way," Celia said.

"It's all right. I want to show you something."

"Please. Let me out."

"Paul and I used to play down here when we were boys."

He went through the gate fast and ran the car along to the mouth of the track through the scrub. He was filled with joy. He felt himself exalted, chosen, advanced upon a path where each step was ordained.

He stopped the car and faced Celia. For a moment—ten seconds or more—they stared at each other. In that time Celia must have passed from simple fright to a knowledge that she was dying. She turned, like some animal from a predator, half hypnotized, and fumbled with the door.

Anger moved my brother at the end. She dared inhabit the same world as our mother. As she got the door open he drew back his arm and struck her on the neck with the edge of his hand. (When we were boys we called this the rabbit punch.) She fell forward, half-way out the door. He got out and ran round to her side. She was speaking in a thin childish voice; an admonition, almost casual in sound. "Stop it. Don't." She put out a hand to hold him off. The slowness of the movement seemed inhuman to him. He caught her hair in both hands and jerked her out of the car and swung her away from it towards the scrub. She stayed on her feet. Her mouth was open and her head lowered. She put a hand to her forehead and brought it away marked with blood. Andrew had strands of hair in his hands. Her hair enraged him. He ran at Celia and struck her on the face; struck her again; and a third time. She fell to the ground and he started to kick her, chest, belly, ribs, with a kind of method. When he stopped she was making bubbling sounds. Her eyes were open. He knelt beside her and put his hands round her throat. His fingers met at the back. He squeezed as hard as he could and felt something in her throat collapse. He kept the pressure up until he was sure she was dead. It was no surprise to him that as she was dying she became ugly.

Andrew stood up. He pulled his fingers straight. He had no fear of being found, but knew he should look about him. Along the low ridge over the creek the houses showed blank faces. Windows were lit by the last rays of the sun. Smoke from a back-yard incinerator hung like mist in a hedge. Only a cat moved, threading delicately through cabbage stumps in a garden.

Andrew knelt down again. He put one arm under Celia's knees and the other under her shoulders. He lifted her up and walked as fast as he could along the path. Ten yards in it narrowed. Her head and feet jammed against stiff manuka twigs. He turned side-on, careful to keep the bloody side of her face away from his jacket. In the clearing he found a gap in the wall large enough to take her. He went down on his knees again and pushed her in. She was very loose and her limbs were difficult to arrange. He put her hands across her chest, then changed them to her sides. He smoothed her skirt, pulled small trees across her, and left without looking back.

At the car Andrew closed the passenger's door, went round to his side, and drove away. He remembered the books falling on the ground. Now they were on the seat. But nothing had to be explained. His part was done. The rest was out of his hands, he could not be responsible. If somebody had come by and put the books on the seat, that must be in the order of things.

He drove at an even pace, filled with a warm and happy lassitude.

He told it in other words, of course. Why should I let him speak?

When he had finished he sat with an earnest expression on his face, as though he had wound up a piece of business. I wondered if he would offer to shake hands. There was no word I could utter. No expression of grief or rage or pity. That could only have been a gift to myself.

"What are you going to do?"

He looked surprised. "Nothing."

"The police are going to catch you."

"I don't see how." He had no interest in this.

"The car," I said. "They're checking registrations. They'll go through every Mini in Auckland."

"Oh."

"They'll get to Mrs. Tillotson."

He made a complete mental retreat; went far away. I kept on talking, though I knew it was useless—my turn now to get through a piece of business. I explained about finger-prints, search, identification. "They'll find the books, wherever you've hidden them. Even if they're burnt they'll find the ashes." Not a flicker of interest from him. I could not believe that during the past week he had not been troubled, back in the territory where the circles overlapped. Now he was safe, at the outer rim.

"What about Jonathan? What about Penny? How do you think they're going to feel?"

He smiled faintly. "You're making a great deal out of nothing."

"Nothing——"

"You don't understand, all that's in the past. Things are different now."

The plan I had made (or grasped) the night before, that mature and final stratagem, came back to me now—a piece of childish wishing. It's hardly surprising that as I'd gone to my pre-den life, to the time of loony John, to pick up my load of responsibility, the solution I'd found should have a boy-scoutish flavour. I seized it now with a passion wholly childish.

"Listen, Andrew. I'll tell you what we're going to do. We're going to go out in that cabin cruiser of yours. This afternoon. We'll say we're going fishing. We'll go out past Rangitoto, right out into the gulf. And then we'll rig up an accident. Those old inboard engines are always exploding. There was a case in the paper only a couple of weeks ago.

We'll start a fire. The whole thing will sink. There won't be anything left. We'll both go down together," I lied. "It'll be quick. It's the best we can do, Andrew. Just you and me together. The police will stop after that. They won't go any further. They can't charge a dead man. It'll be best for Jonathan and Penny.... It's the way Mother would have liked it."

He let me go on, watching in the same blank way; simply recording. The last refinement brought a narrowing to his eyes.

"You're quite mad."

"Andrew, please listen."

"I find it hard to believe you're Mother's son."

"Please——"

"You can't come to arrangements with evil. That's what you've done all your life." Another dialogue was going on. "I was wrong to think I could save you." He was way out on the rim now; the position he had killed Celia from.

I stood up. "I'm ringing the police."

"No, Paul." His voice had a gentle firmness. With a feeling of relief I saw he meant to kill me: he put me back in the world of the sane.

I started for the door. The grief for Celia I had not been able to work up earlier in the morning found an entrance. "You fool," I said, "you bloody maniac. Don't you understand, that girl you killed was worth a dozen times our mother." I stopped at the door. There was something else I had to say. He was on his feet, with the tomahawk in his hand. I knew I could outrun him. Out the back door, over the paddocks. Andrew would never catch me. "Our mother was a stupid bitch," I said.

But at the last his invention outran mine. He threw the tomahawk. I had time only to turn and duck. It struck me on the back, cracking ribs (a wet sound), ploughed a furrow up to my shoulder, and carried on across the side of my head, slicing my ear. I have the impression it then bounced off the door and fell into the broken insides of the record player. I fell down and lay still. Andrew came and stood over me. The wound he had made must have been messy enough to convince him I was dead. He went out of the room and out of the house.

I knew I was badly hurt. There was no feeling in the right side of my back. My face and ear burned as though splashed with acid. At least you tried, I thought—a hysterical response, not the calm one it can sometimes seem to me now. I wondered if I was going to bleed to death. Hurry, I cried, without knowing whom the plea was made to. But there was also an overriding instruction whose source I still do not know: Lie still.

It wasn't over yet.

Andrew came back. He paused to look at me. Then he went to the pile of books in the middle of the room. I heard a grating sound: a tin cap turning. Then the gurgle and splash of liquid. Petrol. Even while I quivered with an increase of terror I was grateful for its sharp reviving smell. The sound went on. It must have been a two-gallon tin. He shifted to the furniture—a soggy sound—then splashed the walls. He should have poured some on me, and put me in my chair to burn. But for this part of the murder I doubt that he had instruction. He screwed the cap back on. Then he came to the door. I heard the rattle of a box of matches.

He struck, threw, ran; never looked back. The room seemed to explode. On my knees, I looked with childish recognition at the yellow viscous liquid that filled it from the windows to the pile of books. A lake of fire. Then I was out of the room, and running down the hall the way a chimpanzee runs, one hand touching the floor; gibbering too like a chimpanzee. I fell into the yard. The pain from my broken ribs made me scream—or perhaps that's imagination. I do remember the idiot clapping of my bone-dry shirts as I went on my simian run under the clothes-line; and my idiot sheep cowering in their corner. It's possible that I saw Andrew's car moving along the road at a speed within the limit, sedate, well bred, away from the burning house, down to the hollow. Certainly I remember it.

I fell on the cold grass and stayed there. I thought with pleasure of my blood seeping into the earth. I have no memory of the firemen coming, or of being carried to the ambulance. But there I remember Farnon; and the relief with which I told him all I knew.

## Epilogue

The police arrested Andrew in his office. He was working on specifications for a retail shop. At the hearing he was found unfit to plead. I don't know where he is now, or in what condition, but it's certain that he'll never be released.

Jonathan wrote me a letter while I was in hospital.

Dear Uncle Paul,

Thank you for trying to help. I'm sorry you got hurt. We are going to live in Australia after the trial. Mum says we'll change our name. She says we're going to forget about the past so I think it will be best if you don't try to find us.

Love and best wishes,
Jonathan

I live in a house by the sea in Nelson Province. It's here I've written this story—cultivating my garden, so to speak. It does not surprise me that what began as the story of Celia's death should have become the story of my life. What could be more natural?

I mourn Celia now and then. But what I really mourn is my books. My poor, burned books. I have orders placed all over the country. The postman curses me.